brush strokes

SARA WETMORE

Book Cover Design by ebooklaunch.com

Print ISBN: 9781737642923

Ebook ISBN: 9781737642930

one

NOTHING PREPARES you for the end of a marriage, yet I feel mine closing all the time. While David is in the office listening to his patients' problems, he ignores mine completely. Probably because he doesn't think they're that serious. But I find myself alone a lot and the nagging thought that somehow I have lost myself will not cease, even when I'm painting a commission or cleaning the house. Especially when I'm painting or cleaning the house.

At least I still have my art, though it hasn't been very expressive in a long time. I spend most mornings working on portraits of families and pets for people who request one from my Etsy shop. I get a surprising amount of business, though I'm sure David would prefer that I not worry myself by monetizing my passion. Not that portraits are my passion. I enjoy abstract oil paintings far more, but I just never seem to have the time or the clarity of mind to produce what I want, which has forced me to abandon my lifelong dream of displaying my art in a gallery and finding buyers with deep pockets that appreciate my art as much as

I do. But I suppose it could be worse. David supports us and I get a little extra money for my rainy day fund.

This lifestyle comes with conditions. Because being a psychiatrist is so stressful (and painting appears so leisurely), David expects me to keep the house in shape. As I navigate all of David's modern furniture in our charming bungalow in Sugar House, Salt Lake City, I feel like a stranger in my own home. I never had a say in how the house was decorated. David already owned the house when we started dating eleven years ago, and when we married when I was twenty-three, I sort of just packed up my clothes and my art supplies and moved in. If it weren't for my large easel in the dining room, where a table should be but isn't, you'd never know that I lived here.

I'm cleaning the house: vacuuming the rugs, wiping dust off of every surface, and finally washing the linens, as I do each month. I enter the bedroom and open the blinds to let a little light in. I don't understand why David likes it so dark all the time.

I throw the comforter onto the floor and begin dismantling the bedsheets. One by one, I remove the pillow cases. I reach across the length of the mattress and grab a corner of the fitted sheet, pulling as I straighten myself, when I see something shiny roll across the white cotton fabric. I pick it up to discover one half of a belly button ring, which confuses me at first because the only piercings I have are in my ears and my nose. Then it hits me. This piece of jewelry belongs to another woman. Another woman has been in my marital bed.

I run to the bathroom, still clutching the belly button ring in my hand, and hurl into the sink. I wipe the vomit from my lips with the back of my hand and look at the jewelry a little closer. It's one diamond set in a circle with a curved silver post sticking out of one side. Where the top piece could be, I have no idea. What matters is that I have found evidence of my husband's infidelity. And yet, I'm not angry.

I leave the jewelry on the counter next to the sink and go to finish washing the sheets. In the meantime, I think of what I want to say to David when he gets home.

IT'S NEARLY dark out when I hear David's keys in the door. I'm sitting stiff and upright on a particularly square black leather armchair, as I have been for an hour, waiting for him to get home. He's late, which considering the body jewelry that is sitting on the small table beside me, isn't that surprising.

The handle turns slowly, as if he is trying to sneak into his own house, and the door creaks as it opens. David doesn't see me as he creeps inside. After all, all of the lights are off in the house. I reach towards the lamp on the table and pull the string to startle him. I've always seen people do that in movies. I couldn't resist.

David jumps a little and then takes a deep breath.

"Oh, it's you. You scared me." He sets his briefcase on the ground and begins removing his shoes.

"Leave those on," I say sternly. He does as he is instructed.

"Okay, what's going on?" he says, his voice edging on caution.

I smile and nod towards the belly button ring on the glass side table. David crosses the room to get a better look.

"What is that?" he asks, squinting his eyes. I suppose it's still a little dark, even with the lamp light throwing shapes and shadows on the walls. I pick up the jewelry and place it in his hand. His face turns white as our linens, which I have since bleached and washed twice.

"How about now? Does it look more familiar?"

I'm enjoying playing with him, watching him squirm like I am a sun child with a magnifying glass and he is an unsuspecting insect.

"You must have just lost this. Remind me, was it missing long?" he lies.

I tilt my head at him and smirk. "David, cut the shit. You and I both know what this is, and that it could not possibly belong to me. Who is she?"

David falls to the floor and the light catches a single tear falling off his clean-shaven cheek. "Her name is Jessica."

He drops the jewelry to the ground. It makes a high-pitched *ping* sound as it makes contact with the dark wooden floors.

"Who is she?" I repeat.

"She's a patient," he confesses.

I should have known. I was a patient of his once, eleven years ago. Once we started dating, I stopped seeing him in a professional capacity. But I should have seen the red flags as brightly then as I do now.

"Jesus Christ, David," I whisper coldly under my breath. "You really have a type, don't you?"

David clutches my leg and begins sobbing. "I'm sorry," he says over and over again. But I'm not listening. Part of me wants to pull him up and comfort him, but then I remember what he has done to me: not just now, but over the last decade. The infidelity, the gaslighting, the domestic prison in which I find myself. I finally see an escape from this life he's built for me, and I'll be damned if he tries to pull me back in.

"Please, can you ever forgive me?" he says, his face slick with tears.

I stare at him, my eyes pinched with disdain. This man didn't just cheat on me. He stole my youth.

"No," I say, "But not for this. For everything."

David hangs his head shamefully. When he looks back up at me, he's crying again.

"We could go to therapy. Couple's therapy. We can work on this. I can be better," he says, gasping for breath between syllables.

"No," I say definitively, "I want a divorce."

At this, David crumples at my feet. Here lies a broken man, but he is insidious and I dare not lay a hand on him. The light. The light beckons me forward and I know I must follow through with this.

"Pack your things. You need to leave," I say.

After a while, David gets up off of the floor and disappears into the bedroom where he packs a garbage bag full of clothes. When he comes back into the living room, he looks dejected and undeniably guilty.

"Where will I go?" he asks.

"Not my problem," I reply icily, "Now give me your key and get out."

David carefully withdraws his keys from his pocket and removes the house key, placing it lightly in my outstretched palm. And just like that, David is gone. My body feels lighter as I watch his car pull out of the driveway and drive off into the night.

DIVORCE IS A BITCH. I served David papers not long after discovering the jewelry in our bed, and it's taken months for him to agree to sign them. I even had to ask for a temporary order for financial support to help out with the bills as I refuse to leave our house after kicking David out. My friend Alice moves in this weekend to rent out the second bedroom—a favor I asked of her knowing that the temporary order would be over soon and then if things went my way and I got the house, I'd be stuck footing the bill with my minimal painting income. Alice kindly agreed since she, like me, is now thirty-three and single.

Alice and I share the same cynical outlook on love. Too many times have we sacrificed ourselves in the name of devotion. In fact, not once have we ever found ourselves in a relationship that didn't require giving up the parts of ourselves that make us whole. Alice is more cynical than I am, however, and I suppose that's why I settled down and she didn't. Whatever the case, she has thrown herself into teaching history at a local high school and working on a nonfiction book about the Cold War in her free time. She's told me about the book half of a dozen times, but I tune out every time she mentions it. History doesn't interest me. I never learn from it anyway.

Today is mine and David's settlement conference with our attorneys. Hopefully now we can finally negotiate a settlement and finalize the judgment of our drawn-out divorce.

I sit in a large conference room in a high-rise building downtown, with floor to ceiling glass windows situated behind me as I watch the door, waiting for David to finally arrive. He's late, as usual. The mediator is here and I plan to sit there until David agrees to give me the only thing that matters to me: the bungalow.

It's hard to say why the bungalow means so much to me when it was David's house to begin with. Even ten years into our marriage and months after I kicked him out, the house is filled with his sleek modern furniture, which has never suited me. But the dining room—the only space that's truly mine—is perfect. I keep bright orange curtains (which David hates) open all day long, exposing the old single-pane windows that wrap around the room with a paint-splattered sheet underneath my easel. The bungalow casts such exquisite light during the day when David is gone and I can open things up. It's ideal for my work.

I also love the bones of the house, its charming potential. I love the location, and with the Salt Lake housing market the way it is, I'd be forced to leave the city if I had to move out. Likely, I'd end up in Moab living in my mother's basement. I couldn't do that. I'd be so far from my friends, from the places I haunt, from the heartbeat of the city itself.

I crave the energy of Sugar House. It's youthful and artistic, a little bit like me, even if I am nearly thirty-four now. I don't feel it. I wake up most days and I feel endless possibilities. I'm not jaded like most people my age. I'm excited about life, especially once I filed for divorce, and I know that optimism and thirst for adventure would fade the second I left Sugar House. Everywhere else is so suburban, with mini-mansions that all look the same spanning from the mountains in the east to the mountains in the west. In Sugar House, each house is old and unique. They're quite a bit smaller and more expensive than the mini-mansions out South, but I could see why. Now that I had been inspired by this town for ten years, I couldn't say goodbye. No. The house would be mine and I would use my rainy day fund (and any money from the divorce settlement) to make it my own. It started with removing David. Next, I would remove all of his stuff.

David walks into the room. He's sweating and a little disheveled. I can tell he doesn't want to be here. He knows what I am asking for and he is still reluctant to agree to my terms. We nod at each other cordially, but there's nothing cordial about this conference. I am out for blood.

"Nice of you to join us, Mr. Grobble," my attorney says, taking a seat after pacing for the last ten minutes.

David doesn't have an attorney. I wonder why. He can certainly afford it. But this bodes well for me. Maybe it's the guilt. I hope it's the guilt.

"Sorry I'm late. Let's get this over with, shall we?" David says, sliding his chair closer to the table and clasping his hands together.

The mediator looks at my attorney and David, displaying how they will be the only ones speaking during this session. I'm only here for intimidation and to see to it that I get what I deserve.

"So, the house appears to be the only property up for debate here," the mediator says calmly. "Ms. Williams says she will not be satisfied without the house."

David anxiously runs his fingers through his hair. "She can have it."

"What?" I blurt out accidentally, forgetting my silent role. "After months of disagreement, what's changed your mind?"

The mediator eyes me in disbelief. After all, I have hired her and my attorney to speak on my behalf.

David lifts his head and stares at me with piercing blue eyes. They are red and swollen like he has been crying.

"I know how much that neighborhood means to you, Emily. I've already found somewhere else to live. It's not worth fighting about anymore."

I'm almost touched by this grand gesture, but then I remember to keep my composure.

"Mr. Grobble, Ms. Williams is prepared to accept your offer," my attorney chimes in. I let out a deep exhale.

My attorney slides a stack of papers towards David, indicating where his signature is required. David signs them without a moment's hesitation.

"Next," my attorney continues, "is the matter of alimony."

The mediator shifts in her seat and looks over her notes. "I believe Ms. Williams is requesting the amount indicated on this form in spousal support. Do you wish to contest?"

David sighs. "Whatever you want, Emily, just take it. I can't go on like this."

My attorney hands David a new stack of papers to sign, which David does hastily before returning the forms for me to sign.

It takes nearly an hour, but we get through all of the papers, and as I sign the last form with a flourish, I realize that this is it. After ten years, David and I are divorced. A burden has been lifted from my shoulders and I sigh, almost feeling guilty for cleaning him out during the so-called negotiations.

The mediator and the attorney shake David's hand goodbye, and just before he leaves, he looks at me with the saddest look in his eyes. They glisten as his eyes well up with tears and he blinks them away. I think of how he sobbed that night when I found the jewelry in our bed and I can't conjure an ounce of tenderness for him.

"Goodbye, Emily," he says.

"Goodbye, David."

And just like that, my new life has begun.

two

IT'S BEEN three months since my divorce was finalized, and I wake up to a strange, boisterous buzzing sound coming from outside. I remember that the landscapers I hired to tear up the yard start today. I meant to wake up before they got here, but I'll admit I've been getting more than enough sleep lately. Too much.

I slip on my jeans that lie draped over the chaise in the bedroom. I sniff the baggy shirt I'm wearing. I haven't showered for two days, but it seems fine enough. I run to the front door and swing it open. I am horrified by what I see.

In the front yard, a crew is cutting down my beloved chokecherry tree that I planted when I first moved into the bungalow, or maybe it was when David and I got married. I can't recall. All I know is that it has been with me for ten years. Ten years, I've watched it grow from a small sapling to a mature, beautiful tree with crimson and auburn leaves that danced when the canyon winds burst down the lanes lower in the valley. I'd observe it when I drank my morning coffee on the porch swing as the sun rose in the east, and later, I'd examine it even closer as it reflected the warm pink and cool purple sunsets in the west. And now, its severed limbs are falling to the ground, one by one, leaving a naked trunk with just a few remaining limbs sticking out of the ground.

Furious, I run to the man guiding the crew. He is very tall, with a bushy beard and long dark hair pulled back into a man-bun. He wears a red plaid shirt, and his thick, muscular arms are bursting out of the sleeves as he points to the next tree limb to sacrifice.

"Stop! Stop! Stop!" I scream over the humming saws.

The man yells for the crew to stop and suddenly I am made aware of how quiet the morning is.

"Aye?" the man asks.

"Look what you've done to my tree!" I say, fighting back tears. "It's ruined."

"Jist daein' uir jobs, miss." His accent is odd. I can't place it. Somewhere in the UK. Ireland? Scotland, perhaps?

"I was very specific about tearing up everything but the tree!" I shout.

The man instructs his men to take a quick break and pulls me aside so that we can talk in the shade.

"Look, there's nae need tae gie angry. Thes tree is sick. By aw accoonts, it's awreddy deid," he says.

I rub the temples of my head. I can't believe what I am hearing. "It seemed fine to me. You have no right to just hack down this tree!"

The man shifts his legs and straightens up. I didn't realize how tall he is.

"Ye see 'at canker thaur? Did ye notice hoo th' limbs leaned? Hoo th' leaves ur discolored? Fur Christ's sake, thaur ur mushrooms growin' coz th' damned hin' is deid! Thes tree was a hazard. We ur daein' ye a favur."

I ponder this. I had noticed these things, but I admittedly don't know much about trees. The tree seemed fine to me. Healthy, even. I've never been good at reading the signs.

"You should have at least talked to me about this first," I say stubbornly.

"Ah tried knockin' oan yer duir, miss. Thaur was nae answer. Th' way Ah see it, thes tree was comin' doon wi' ur withit uir help. Sae, ah pit mah men tae wark."

I look at the half-sawed tree and a sadness washes over me. He must have been able to tell because he set his palm on my shoulder.

"Listen, when we ur plantin', we'll pit a new tree in its place. Diz 'at soond aw reit?" he says in a calm, level voice.

"Fine," I say, shrugging his hand off of me. "But any more decisions like this have to go by me first, is that clear?"

The man bows but I can't tell if he's patronizing me.

"Yer wish is mah commain," he says with a hint of sarcasm.

I shove him. "You don't need to be such a dick about it," I say, turning around to go back inside.

"Nur dae ye need tae be sic' a bitch," he mutters softly, but I hear him, and for an instant, my head is spinning and I feel a primal rage bubble up inside me. I have two choices: I can ignore him and go back inside, make some coffee, and calm down; or I could turn around and take out the last eleven years of frustration that I've been holding inside on the landscaper. For some inexplicable reason, I choose the latter.

"Listen, you piece of shit," I begin, stomping my way

toward the man in red like I am the bull and he is the matador, "I employ you. I will rate your company when you are done. And if I am not satisfied—which I assure you, right now I am not—you'll be packing up to wherever you came from because you won't work a day in Utah ever again. Do I make myself clear?"

The man's face sinks in shame. "Crystal clear, miss."

And then he turns around and gets back to work.

I take my cue to leave and go back inside. But I can't stop watching the man in red. He works with such authority that I begin to feel bad about my outburst. He clearly knows better than I do about these kinds of things—trees, flowers, earth—and I had no right to raise such a commotion. I know I crossed the line when I said I would get him fired and deported. That wasn't me. I have no idea where this monster came from.

I suppose money has been tight lately, even with the alimony payments from David, even with Alice moving in and helping with the mortgage, and even with commissions from my Etsy shop coming in droves. I have no desire to work unless it is a larger commission, so I'm not making as much as I probably can. Something is weighing on me, but I can't tell what it is. So, I stand in front of the window, drink my coffee, and watch the landscapers destroy the last piece of the past.

Alice wakes up late, as usual. She is done teaching for the school year and is off for the summer. All those early mornings, the ones I couldn't bear myself, must have caught up with her because now she spends her mornings asleep and her nights awake working on her book about the Cold War.

She pours herself a cup of coffee, scratching her short

matted hair, and joins me by the window. She sees what I see, but I doubt she feels what I feel.

"Everything okay? I heard yelling," she says.

I sigh. "Is anything ever okay?"

Alice rubs my back gently as we watch the last of the tree come down.

"Change is hard," she says, "But we'll get through it."

I take her hand and squeeze it tight. "Thanks, Alice."

We stand there watching the landscapers for a while longer. The man in red is starting to pack up tools in the trailer hitched to a white pickup truck parked on the street.

"That one's kind of cute," Alice says, interrupting our silence.

"Who?" I say, intrigued. I step closer to the glass, observing the five men in my yard. Some are old, some are young. But only one of them stands out among the rest.

"The lumberjack. Mmm-mmm-mmm." she says. I can't tell if she's savoring the man or the coffee.

"Him?" I respond, dumbfounded, "You can't be serious. He's just a bumbling meathead with a man-bun. Besides, he's not exactly your type."

"But he's totally yours," Alice quips.

I blush. "Maybe in my twenties. Men like that need to grow up. What is he, nearly forty?"

"You must be forgetting that older men are sort of your type, too."

She's right. I had jumped into a relationship with David even though he was eleven years older than me, and within a year, we were married. David didn't have a man-bun though, and he certainly wouldn't be caught wearing red plaid like some hipster. He was clean cut, clean shaven, and always sharp-dressed. I think Alice would agree that David was wrong for me for a lot of reasons. Our clashing styles were just one piece of the puzzle.

I've never conformed to one style. I value comfort over fashion, but one thing Alice knows about me is that I wouldn't be caught dead in a suit, and I avoid corporate colors like black and navy. My wardrobe is colorful and whimsical. I love tye-dye and mandalas. Bright colors that demand to be seen. Maybe because I felt so invisible all the time.

I nudge Alice with my elbow and she spills a bit of her coffee over David's white rug.

"Sorry, I didn't mean—"

"No," I say, "It's fine. I should probably get rid of it anyway." And with that, I take a peek into my mug and dump the remaining coffee onto the floor, leaving a large dark stain on David's rug. I smile to myself, knowing I'll throw that in the dumpster down the street later that day. While I am focused on renewing the front yard, I know I need to focus inward and clear out the rest of David's furniture if I want a fresh start.

Alice laughs with me, and before I know it, she's helping me pull the rug out from underneath the furniture and rolling it up to throw outside.

"One less piece of David," Alice says, nodding in approval.

"One hundred more to go."

ONE BY ONE, Alice and I carry pieces of David's furniture out to her truck and fit in as much as we can. Alice says she'd be happy to drop them off at the Goodwill later that day, though I know she's just looking for excuses not to write.

With my living room nearly bare, I feel excited by the blank slate. I decide I'll join Alice on her trip to the Goodwill to see if there is any eclectic furniture that I can take home to fill the empty space.

But first, I need to get some painting done. There's a commission I've been sitting on for nearly a week that I have only started sketching, and the customer wants it as soon as possible. It's a portrait of a dog that has recently died. It makes me sad to work on it, knowing what has been and what is no longer, but I'm happy to offer this service. I get so many commissions for portraits of dead pets. I never turn them down because while I've never had a pet myself, I know what it's like to lose someone close to you. My dad died when I was twenty-one. Heart attack.

Maybe it's just the artist in me talking, but it's nice to have something more than a photograph to remember them by. There's something about having someone meticulously paint your loved ones with small strokes, brush by brush, dab by dab, until what they are presented with is a permanent fixture in their homes that captures the essence of who the subject once was.

I carefully finish sketching the outline for the dog painting. At this stage, it looks totally underwhelming. Like a line drawing of any dog you can conjure in your mind. Without the texture of paint, it is hard to see what the dog represents. I always ask my customers what their pets were like so that I don't go into it blindly. I need to know them, *really* know them, before I can even think about dipping my brush into my oil paints.

This seems like a good stopping point, so I interrupt

Alice's writing time to see if she wants to make the trip, to which she happily obliges.

I climb into the front passenger seat of her black F-350, trying to ignore the hole in my front yard where the chokecherry tree once stood. Thinking about the tree just gets me riled up again. But deep down, I know I am in the wrong. Wasn't it Fitzgerald that once wrote, "Beautiful things grow to a certain height and then they fail and fade off, breathing out memories as they decay?" The tree is no exception, and it dawns on me that I owe the landscapers a huge apology.

"We'll plant something even better," Alice says, noticing my discomfort.

"That's what the lumberjack said," I say. "It's hard letting go."

"True," she says, putting the truck in reverse and pulling out of the driveway, "But think of it like a new beginning. We're doing that now with David's stuff, and we'll do it with the front yard, too. It's okay to mourn the past, but don't let it stop you from living a fulfilling life."

She's right. Why is she always right? So much wisdom trapped inside one so small.

WE ARRIVE at the Goodwill and I leave Alice to deal with unloading the truck with the attendant. I am driven with purpose as I enter the doors and behold all of the wonderful old things that people have abandoned.

I walk toward the back of the store where they display the furniture and I am taken by a light green sofa with ornate wooden accents. I take a seat on it, even though customers really aren't allowed to, and imagine what it would look like in my living room. I picture it against the wall with some of my more colorful art pieces hanging above it and a brand new turquoise rug (which I will search for on the internet as soon as I get home). In my imagination, my entire house is transformed and suddenly, I am inspired and happy.

I reach for the tag and find its price agreeable. I just need Alice's help getting it home. I just pray that it will fit in her truck bed. Without hesitation, I approach the checkout and buy the sofa before running out to Alice and telling her the good news.

"Are you sure it will fit?" she says dubiously.

"Yes," I lie, "I mean, I didn't measure it, but it should be fine."

The attendant, Alice, and I all carry the sofa out to the truck and it is monstrously heavy. We carry it up a ramp and set it down in the truck bed. Alice can't close the tailgate, but we secure the sofa with lots of straps and agree to drive especially slow.

It's only a few blocks from the house so we get there without any issues. But when we go to unload the truck, we realize that we need a third person to lift it.

"Fuck," I say, setting down one end of the sofa for the dozenth time. "Who can we ask to help us?"

"Those landscapers will be back in the morning, right?" says Alice.

I shoot her an angry look, "Alice, no."

"I'm sure they'd be happy to help. There's no harm in asking."

I think about asking the man in red. I know I'll need to apologize first, but the thought of admitting I was wrong makes me sick. Still, Alice makes a good point, and I don't know anyone else that I could call.

"Fine," I say, "It will have to do."

We climb out of the truck and I continue walking down the street as Alice unlocks the front door.

"Where are you going?" she asks.

"To get some beer."

three

I WAIT for the man in red and his crew to finish up for the day. The tree is completely gone now. I thought I would still be angry; perhaps even angrier seeing nothing but a hole in the ground where my young chokecherry tree once stood. But instead I see what that horrible man was saying. I hadn't been able to see it before, but he was right, it was dead, even if it still grew sickly leaves.

Now, I am energized by the progress they have made on my yard. In just two short days, they have completely dug up every square inch surrounding the front of the bungalow. Even though I'm not designing the new yard, my mind is alive with possibilities. Suddenly, I am struck by the intense desire to be part of the designing process. But I know that's not possible. The man in red already has plans of his own.

As the men are packing up, I run out to the street and shout at the lumberjack. He's wearing green plaid today, so I suppose I have to come up with a new nickname for him, or rather, it is time for proper introductions besides "dick" and "bitch."

"Hey, I'm nae lookin' fur trooble," he murmurs behind his thick brown beard.

I place my hands on my hips. "Trouble? No, no. I was hoping you had time to come sit with me, maybe talk over some beers?"

He pauses for a long time. Then, his mouth peels into a wide grin and he outstretches his hand, "Aye, I'd loch 'at very much. I'm Roban, by th' way."

"Emily," I say, shaking his hand. His grip is tight and strong. "Will your guys be all right heading out without you?"

"Och, aye, They'll be fine. Ah can jist caa an Uber. Nae worries."

I lead him up the steps of the front porch and sit down on one of the two Adirondack chairs facing the street. Between them sits a small cooler which I have presumptuously filled with ice and beer while the men were working earlier. I had hoped he would agree to sit with me so I could properly apologize, despite my horrible outburst the day prior. And maybe, just maybe, he could help Alice and I move the couch inside.

Roban takes a seat beside me and leans back, placing his hands leisurely behind his head.

"Admiring your work?" I say, hiding a smile.

"It diz feel guid tae see it frae yer perspectife."

I open the cooler and offer him a beer. He reaches for an amber ale and I take a sour ale, even though there are IPAs. Why did I buy so many IPAs? I don't like them and he seems not to either. Everyone knows they taste like grass. Oh well. I am relieved that he even agreed to sit down with me.

I take a deep breath as a silence takes us and there's nothing we can hear except the afternoon birds chirping in the summer sun. "Listen, I wanted to apologize about yesterday. I know you were right about the tree, it was just a lot for me to process. I planted that tree myself when I moved here, and—"

"I'm sorry Ah called ye a bitch," he says. He scratches his head and runs his fingers through his hair, evading my gaze.

My initial impulse is to tell him to go to hell, but I remember that I am trying to be mature about this, and I still haven't quite finished my own apology.

"Thank you," I say, surprising even me. "I'm sorry I called you a dick."

Roban laughs a deep, hearty laugh, and soon, I find myself nervously laughing with him.

"Ah can't believe ye did 'at," he says.

"Did what? Call you a dick?"

"Aye," he says, "Ah didn't expect sae much venom from... weel, a hen loch ye."

I feel myself getting defensive again. "What is that supposed to mean?"

"Ah don't ken," Roban says, "Ye an' yer hippie pajamas. Ah guess it seems loch yoo'd be more... zen."

I nearly choke on my beer. "Zen is not the word I would use to describe me."

Roban smiles at me, and I can't tell if it's the beer working overtime or if he's making me blush.

"Hoo woods ye describe yerself 'en?" he says, taking a long sip of his amber ale.

"You'll just have to find out."

What am I saying? Am I flirting with the landscaper? What if Alice was right and he is my type? Fuck. No, I'm not doing this again. I compose myself and shake out my hair. I can feel Roban's eyes on me, but I try to ignore it.

"Aw reit 'en, I'm game," he says.

I feel exposed and I don't like it. I need to take control of this interaction quickly, or else he just might end up inside with me, his green plaid shirt draped across my chaise in the bedroom.

"Tell me about you," I say, trying to steer the conversation away from me and inevitably my failed marriage. "What brought you to Utah?"

I hoped I didn't sound too xenophobic. I was merely curious why someone from overseas would find a new home in a place like Salt Lake City. Yes, the mountains are gorgeous and our deserts are spectacular, but everything else is so mundane. Maybe it's just because I've lived here my whole life. I take the natural splendor around me for granted.

"Honestly?" he says.

"Honestly," I repeat.

He rocks a little in his seat and fidgets with the label on the beer bottle. I'm dying to hear what he has to say.

"It was a lifelang dream efter Ah reid *Desert Solitaire* by Edward Abbey at uni. 'En when mah engagement was called aff, Ah needed tae escape. Ah figured Ah micht as well come haur an' see th' lain Edward Abbey professed tae loove sae much. 'En Ah ne'er left," Roban says, chuckling. He glides his hand through his hair and fixes his bun.

"I didn't peg you as much of a reader," I say, eyes wide in surprise.

Roban gasps and takes a long swig of his beer. "Ah reid constantly. Mainly poetry. Ah guess 'at micht surprise fowk, but it inspires me."

"That's how I feel about art," I say.

"Didn't peg ye as much ay an artist," Roban laughs, "Althoogh th' paint oan yer clothes makes a lot mair sense noo. Whit dae ye paint?"

I tell him about my Etsy commissions and even show him a few photos on my phone. He seems genuinely interested, which is rare for me. Usually, people's eyes gloss over when I start talking about my art. No one seems to care about art anymore.

"Sae, whit dae ye *want* tae paint?" Roban asks.

The question surprises me. I don't have an answer prepared. In truth, I think about it all the time but have never been prompted to put it into words. How do I vocalize my dream without sounding silly? I take a deep breath and sip from my sour ale, lips puckering from the taste.

"I want to be able to shut down the Etsy shop and make enough money from my abstract oil paintings. Maybe have them displayed in a gallery somewhere. Unfortunately, the art scene here is pretty much nonexistent." I sigh. "It's fine though. Who else can say they are a professional painter? It beats having to sell my soul to some corporation by becoming a graphic designer. I am blessed to have so many commissions. Really, I make it sound worse than it is."

Roban looks off into the yard and squints as a cloud drifts past, sunlight beaming onto the porch. "Ah kin 'at. Ah rilly dae."

I'm puzzled for a moment. "What do you mean?"

He leans forward and rests his elbows on his knees. "That's wa Ah chose tae be a landscaper. 'At, an' it's hard tae gie a wark visa. Ah wanted tae be close tae th' earth. Ah was gardener back in Oban an'—"

"Wait a minute. Your name is Roban and you're from a place called Oban? Roban from Oban?" I nearly choke on my beer, I am laughing so hard.

Roban's cheeks burst into crimson. "Aye. Ah gie 'at a lot. It's jist a coincidence. Truly."

"I'm sorry," I say, stifling my laughter. The shifting color of his face makes me feel bad for cracking up. "Please continue. You were a gardener in Oban, and then what?"

Roban eyes me incredulously. "Life happened. An' 'en Ah suppose life didn't happen. Ah got mah degree in horticulture hopin' tae become a botanist, but it turns it thaur isn't much demain fur 'at. Sae, Ah moved an' joined a landscapin' company haur."

I remember how he mentioned a broken off engagement earlier. I wonder if that's what he meant by "life didn't happen." I feel sorry for him, but also, I think I understand what he's been through. We've all loved and lost. Although, depending on his circumstances, it's possible that losing his loved one hurt more than losing David.

"I'm sorry," I say.

"Sorry fur whit?" Roban's face twists and he's raising his left eyebrow at me.

"Sorry about life. Not happening, that is. You don't need to give me the details." Though I am intensely curious, I hide that from Roban. I'm working on being more polite, less brazen, but I find myself struggling to contain the words. "Unless you want to."

Fuck. There I go, overreaching again. I know it's none of my business, and I'm sure Roban knows that, too. Yet, still, he bewilders both of us when he opens his mouth to speak.

"There's nae much tae teel, rilly," Roban says, his eyes drooping, "Ah thooght Ah mit mah soolmate at uni. We waur together fur a lang time. It jist seemed natural tae gie married. Sae, we got engaged. But jist a few weeks before th' weddin', Sophie got scared. Ah tried tae wark on it wi' 'er, but ultimately, she said she needed tae experience th' warld before she settled doon. 'Er words, nae mine."

Roban clears his throat and sniffles. It's hard for him to talk about, and I can tell he's trying not to cry. I never expected such a big man to be so sensitive. But then again, he reads poetry, so perhaps I shouldn't be so astonished.

I set my hand on his knee and he looks up at me, his icy blue eyes still languorous. The corner of his mouth coils, and he sets his hand on mine. We sit there, not saying a word, just looking at each other straight in the eyes for a long time. Too long. Roban leans in towards my face and I feel like I might faint. Like a deer in the headlights, I freeze, unable to lean in myself and incapable of leaning back like I know I should. I close my eyes gently and wait for him to kiss me.

I am shocked by the feeling of his big clumsy fingers pinching the skin near my eye.

"Ouch! What the hell?" I shout.

Roban extends his finger toward me, revealing a small black eyelash. My eyelash.

How could I be so stupid, to think that a man like Roban would ever be interested in me! The point was moot anyway. After my divorce was finalized, I decided that I would live my life for me, on my terms. Romance would only get in the way of that.

I take a deep breath and blow the eyelash off the tip of his finger. It's best that things remain platonic between us. Definitely.

Roban smiles and polishes off the rest of his beer. He's rising from his seat when we both hear a peculiar noise, almost like a baby crying, but smaller. So much smaller. Alarmed, I stand up, too, and glance at Roban. His eyes are shifting around the demolished yard until they land on the hedges separating my property from my neighbor's.

He motions for me to follow him, and together, we

follow the crying sound on tiptoes all the way to the hedge. Roban slowly kneels down in the dirt and reaches his arm into the shrubbery. When he retracts his arm, I am awed by the small creature held lightly in his hand: a small black kitten.

Roban holds the kitten to his chest and begins stroking its head and chin, urging the little one to stop crying. Gradually, its cries become less frequent, and soon it is quietly resting against his chest as he looks it over, searching for possible injuries.

"Seems braw, but thaur aren't any siblings ur its mammy nearby. It needs tae be taken tae a vet an' homed if it's gonnae survife. It's far tay yoong tae survife it haur alone," he says, handing the kitten to me.

Reluctantly, I pick it up. "Roban, I can't..." I begin, but the kitten looks up at me with big gold eyes and I can't help but fall under its spell. "I've never had a pet before. What should I do?"

Roban rapidly lists all of the things I'll need from Petco, but I'm distracted by this living, breathing thing in my arms.

"What's yer number? I'll jist text ye th' list sae ye don't forgit anythin'," he says.

I don't think twice. I just recite my number aloud and wait for the vibration of Roban's text message in my back pocket.

"Sent! Noo gang gie th' supplies an' 'en tak' it tae th' vet as suin as ye can. It micht need medical attention. It's stoaner tae say, I'm nae expert."

I ignore him as I stare into the creature's eyes. It blinks slowly at me, relaxing in my grasp. I kiss it on the head and rock my torso from side to side like I'm coddling an infant.

"Are you sure you can't take it?" I say, though secretly I'm hoping he declines.

"Aye. Ah jist rent a room in a hoose in Glendale. Th' owner doesn't allaw pets," he says, an edge of disappointment in his voice. But I'm elated to hear it, even though I never intended to have a pet.

I wonder how this is going to impact my independence. Fortunately, Alice lives with me now and can help take care of the cat when I'm busy, exhausted, or out of town. This lightens my heart a bit and sweetens me toward the kitten even more.

"I guess I better get going," I say, clutching the kitten to my chest.

"Yoo're reit," Roban says. reaching toward me and petting the kitten. "Ah guess I'll see ye next week when we gie started oan layin' doon th' rock?"

The thought of waiting until next week to see him again fills me with a dreadful sensation. I can't place it, but part of me wants him to stay. But I know better than that. Nothing comes between me and my art. And once this yard is finished and the house is empty, I can begin my new life for real: just me (occasionally Alice) and my paint brushes versus the world.

"I'd shake your hand, but you know," I say, nodding toward the kitten. "It was really nice talking to you. And again, sorry about my temper. I'll try to be pleasant from here on out, but no promises."

Roban laughs. "Until we meit again," he says, bowing awkwardly, and then he walks down the sidewalk toward the center of Sugar House. I don't ask if I can call him an Uber. I just stand there, a wriggly kitten in my arms, watching him walk away. I completely forget to ask about moving the couch.

four

THE VET SAYS the kitten is in perfect health, despite desperately needing food and water. The vet also determines that this kitten is, in fact, a girl and not a boy like I had initially suspected. We run some errands to pick up everything the creature needs to make a home in the bungalow. As I am selecting a variety of toys, a young woman in her twenties dips in front of me, letting out a prolonged "Awww" as she eyes the kitten in my arms.

"What's its name?" she says. The question catches me off guard. I haven't given her a name yet. Rather than admitting this, I announce the first name that comes to mind.

"Vanta," I say.

"Vanta?" the girl says, wrinkling her nose.

"Yeah, like Vantablack. It's one of the darkest shades of black known to man."

"Oh, cool!" she says, stroking the kitten behind the ears. "Thanks for letting me say hi to your cat." And just like that, she walks away.

Vanta, I think. *I like it.*

Vanta and I head home with our bounty. I admit that I might have bought way more than a cat needs, but never having had a pet before, I panicked and picked up everything the internet suggested I could possibly use.

Alice helps me bring in all of the pet stuff and goes completely ga-ga over our new housemate.

"I'm glad you decided to keep her instead of Mr. Manbun," she says.

"His name is Roban," I correct her.

"You named the cat Roban? What kind of name is that?"

"No," I say, sighing deeply, "The cat's name is Vanta. Mr. Manbun's name is Roban. It's Scottish or something."

Alice smirks at me. "You like him!"

"I do not. Shut up." I feel my face bloom.

"If you say so," she says, casting me an overexaggerated wink. "I grabbed the mail. It's over there on the counter."

I approach the pile of mail, but as I hold each envelope, I can't escape this uneasy feeling. I know most of these envelopes contain a bill. One that I am not entirely prepared to pay. I open the top envelope. It's my mortgage bill. Even though it's the same every month, it still surprises me every time. Alice pays more than her fair share, and even with alimony checks, I find myself pooling pennies to pay it every month. Being a painter, and only a painter, has its downsides.

"Fuck," I mumble under my breath, immediately regretting how much I bought at the pet store.

"Emily, what is it?" Alice asks.

"It's nothing," I lie. I know that if I tell the truth, Alice will just try to help. The last thing I want is to be someone's charity case. This is *my* house now. I need to find a way to keep up with the payments. I had been planning on taking money out of savings to pay the landscapers, and even that is almost enough to run me dry. I'm desperate for a miracle.

I feel my phone buzz and realize I have a new request from my Etsy shop. It's from a woman named Margaret Conway. To my surprise, she has purchased my largest size of oil painting, which no one ever does. Probably because no one wants to drop a couple grand on a piece of art when a photograph does just as well. Not so with Margaret Conway.

In her notes, she says she will pay double if I can finish the painting and ship it out within a week. *One week.* The thought is daunting but I can hardly deny the opportunity to make twice as much on my most profitable product, especially considering my financial predicament. Fortunately, Margaret has left her phone number so we can discuss the project. It's late, so I make a reminder on my phone to call her in the morning. Maybe she can be flexible. Even if I stayed up all night every night, I don't know that I would be able to paint a forty-seven inch by fifty-five inch portrait in one week. But I would certainly try.

After getting ready to sleep, I grab Vanta and set her upon my bed.

"You can sleep here if you want," I say aloud, as if the kitten can understand me.

Instead, Vanta hops right off the bed and exits the room. I'm a little hurt by her rejection, but I respect her autonomy. I guess you can't force a cat to do anything it doesn't want to.

———

"MARGARET?" I say into the phone's receiver. "It's Emily Williams from Etsy. I was hoping to discuss your recent request."

There is a brief silence on the other line.

"Oh, yes. From Etsy," she mumbles to herself, though I can hear every word. She sounds old and a little senile, but a customer is still a customer. "I was hoping you could deliver a portrait of my husband and I within a week's time. I know this is a big request, but I need it in time for our fifty-fifth wedding anniversary."

I want to help her, I truly do. How touching for her to want to immortalize their lifelong partnership with a painting. And of all the painters out there, she chose me. That has to mean something. But a week still seems like too large of an ask, so I begin my negotiations.

"That's the thing," I say, my voice trembling just a little, "I don't think I could get this done in a week even if I give it my undivided attention. Perhaps two weeks would be more reasonable?"

I remember that I need the money within the next several weeks for my mortgage payment, so I hope she can be flexible. I want to finish the project and collect my money just as quickly as she wants her gift.

"Two weeks, you say?" Margaret says, slowly mulling it over. "It will be tight. Do you think you can do overnight shipping?"

"Yes, absolutely," I say, completely relieved. "I can get started on it this afternoon if you send me the photograph you'd like me to use for reference."

Margaret agrees to email me the photo and thanks me for agreeing to such a quick turnaround. I am thankful for her business, more so than my usual commissions, and for once I don't feel stressed about money.

• • •

IT'S afternoon and I begin sketching the broader details of Margaret and her husband, who I learn is named Charles. The reference photo is from their wedding day fifty-five years prior, so I can't glean as many fine lines from the photo as I'd like. It presents a unique challenge, but one that I am determined to overcome.

As I am sketching, I am distracted by the crew of men laying out the irrigation for my new yard, including Roban. Today, he's forgone his usual plaid button up shirts for a black t-shirt, which pulls a little tight across his brawny chest. So, I alternate between lightly penciling the smiling faces of Margaret and Charles Conway and staring out the window, observing the work being done. We both make incremental progress, which I love to see. In fact, watching Roban hard at work in the heat only pushes me to work harder, sketch faster, until the groundwork is nearly complete.

Still, I can feel myself getting distracted, like perhaps if I sketched somewhere else I could be much more productive. Roban is so annoying. I hate the fact that he's been on my mind all day and that even when I am working, his presence cannot be avoided.

Vanta climbs up my pant leg, which hurts like hell, but she's so cute I just scoop her up and take a seat with her on my lap. I pet her and she purrs, so I guess I am doing this whole pet ownership thing right. She claws up my hands as I try to tickle her belly the way I've seen countless others do in online videos. She doesn't look surprised when I abruptly lift my hand, but I keep doing it anyway because I find the softness of her fur to be calming.

Yet, even while playing with Vanta, my mind inevitably

evokes Roban and how we found the kitten together and how he practically forced me to take her. I am only in this situation because of him. Now, another living, breathing creature depends on me to live and I don't know if I can handle the pressure. Yes, she is impossibly cute, like a little baby fruit bat or a soot sprite in a Miyazaki film, but it is not lost on me that she depends on me more than I depend on her. Regardless, it's only been a day, but I feel this acute sensation that I truly love her.

THE SETTING SUN casts a pink glow through the open windows, which signals to me that I should probably stop sketching for the day. Though, two weeks... I sigh. Two weeks is not a lot of time to finish this painting. I need to focus. No more distractions.

The doorbell rings, striking panic in my bones. No one ever rings the doorbell unless it's a delivery man dropping off an expensive package or someone soliciting fiber-optic internet or the Mormon religion. I find it best to ignore my doorbell for this reason. Still, I'm curious, so I take out my phone and open up the Nest app to see who's there.

I am surprised, elated, and also a little bit annoyed to see Roban waiting patiently on my porch, holding a six-pack in his right hand. I see the white truck with the huge trailer that usually parks out front during the day when the crew is working on the yard is gone. They must have left him behind. So, I take a deep breath and open the door.

"Emily," Roban says sheepishly, staring down at his fidgeting feet. "Ah was hopin' ye micht hae a beer wi' me?"

With him standing there, stranded and trembling, I could scarcely refuse. It was like adopting an abandoned kitten all over again, only this time, I was letting a burly Scotsman into my home.

"Come on in, it's too hot outside."

I lead him to the living room where Alice is reading a book. She eyes Roban up and down, shuts her book, and leaves, nudging me with her elbow as she exits without saying a word.

"Sorry about her. That's my friend, Alice. She lives here."

"Och, nae an amicable type, is she?" Roban says, handing me a beer. I take it from his large hand and take a seat on the couch. Roban remains standing, observing my lack of decor.

"She can be a bit prickly."

The truth was that Alice liked Roban from the first moment she saw him. Not for her, but for me. A point once again made obviously clear when she nudged me on her way out. I resent it, yet I keep finding myself softening toward Roban despite my efforts to stay uninvolved.

As Roban looks around the room, which is largely empty except for the couch that I got at the thrift store (which finally made its way inside thanks to a little bit of help from my neighbor), his eyes stop on the giant canvas resting upon my easel in the dining room. He approaches it slowly, as if trying not to spook a wild animal.

"Did ye draw thes?" he says, gesturing toward my sketch of Margaret Conway and her husband. At first, I'm a little embarrassed, but seeing as it's just a sketch, I am not expecting any praise or criticism.

"Yeah," I say, twirling my brown hair in my fingers. "I've been at it all day."

"It's huge!" he exclaims. "Ye did aw ay thes in a day?"

I shrug my shoulders nonchalantly. "I sketch fast, what can I say?"

Roban stares at it for a long time before he returns to the living room and takes a seat beside me. I can feel heat radiating from his body, making me acutely aware of how close we are to touching.

"It's a painting I've been commissioned to do. This woman wants a portrait of her and her husband for their fifty-fifth anniversary," I explain.

"It's impressife. Ah ken ye mentioned ye waur an artist, but Ah didn't realize hoo skilled ye ur. Ah thooght ye jist meant it as a—"

"A hobby?" I interrupt him, a sharp edge in my voice.

"Ah didn't mean it loch 'at," he says, looking down at his hands cupping a full can of beer.

I dismiss the jab at my career. I get it all the time. People find it hard to believe that someone can make a living as an artist of any kind. I didn't mean to make Roban feel bad about it, but I do want to be taken seriously. Instead of inciting an argument, I reluctantly decide to open up, to let him into my world.

"I'm dreading the part where I put paint to canvas," I confess, "I have a reference photograph, but I want it to properly convey their love for each other, seeing as it's an anniversary present."

"Can Ah see it?" Roban asks.

"See what?"

"Th' photograph."

I set my beer down on the coffee table and take out my phone to pull up the photo of Margaret and Charles in my inbox. I hand it to Roban, our fingers slightly grazing each other. Roban looks at it for a moment or two before handing it back to me and staring off into space.

"Th' desert is a paradise, if thou wert there, if thou wert there," Roban says, his voice lilting over each word.

"That's beautiful. What is that? A song?" I ask.

"Nae," Roban says, "It's frae a poem by Rabbie Burns called. 'O, Wert Thou in the Cauld Blast.'"

"What prompted that?"

Roban smirks, his lips curling on just the right side of his face, "I'm simply inspired by their loove. It's quite apparent in th' photae, don't ye hink?"

I look at the photo once more. "I guess they do look clearly in love, but I can't place why."

Roban leans in close to me to get a better look at the photograph. "Weel, first, ye must look at their eyes. they ur slightly creased, loch they're smilin' aw by themselves. 'En there's their proximity tae one anither. See hoo ye cooldn't fit a feaither atween them, they're holdin' each other sae close?"

As he speaks, I'm looking at Roban instead of the photo: his long flowing hair, the strength of his bearded jaw, the weathered nature of his sun-kissed skin. He looks up at me and we lock eyes, stuck in a trance that I can't shake.

"What else?" I whisper.

"Th' husband is also protectin' his wife. Whether he is conscioos ay it ur nae, he is standin' oan th' side closest tae th' street sae 'at she doesn't gie hurt. An' their bodies ur open, showin' their comfort wi' one anither."

I lean in closer to him. "And?"

"Most ay aw there's thes intangible spark 'at one can only see if they feel it."

His face is hovering centimeters away from my own. I can feel his warm breath on my lips. My eyelids flutter down and for a minute I think I'm going to kiss him until I realize what is happening.

Hastily, I stand up and stuff my phone back in my pocket, twirling my hair forward as if it could cover my blushing face. Roban looks shocked like he had been thinking what I was thinking, feeling what I was feeling.

"I'm sorry," I say, my voice breaking. "Can you excuse me for just a second? I need to... tend to something. I'll be right back."

I leave Roban alone and bewildered in my living room while I go to the bathroom and splash some cold water on my face.

Stop. I think to myself. *Stop this right now.* I can't deny that I feel something with Roban, but I'm newly divorced and just discovering myself for the first time. I'm learning to take care of myself and to be comfortable being alone. And honestly, these months since the divorce have been the happiest, most liberating in my life. I can't let anyone interfere with that. Not even Roban.

I cautiously enter the living room and Roban is still sitting there, fiddling his thumbs.

"Sorry, I—" I begin, trying to conjure up a lie, but I am immediately interrupted by Roban.

"Look. Ah didn't mean tae scare ye," he says, "Ah like ye, Emily. A lot. Ah hink yoo're bonnie, talented, an' if i'm bein' honest, a wee terrifyin'. But if ye don't feel th' sam, Ah kin. I'll finish yer yard an' ne'er speak tae ye again if that's whit ye want."

My eyes widen and become glossy like glass as I quickly blink away tears.

"I don't know what I want," I say, rubbing my forehead. "I think I just need to focus on my art right now. I can't get involved, even with someone as wonderful as you."

There is a pause between us and I am fully expecting

Roban to get up and leave, but instead he cracks a smile and says, “Ye hink I’m wonderful?”

He completely misses the point, and suddenly I feel very hot and itchy.

“No— I mean, yes. That’s irrelevant. I need to focus, Roban, and I can’t do that with you around, so will you please just leave.”

I gesture toward the door and he rises from the couch, leaving the beer on the table.

“I’ll dae as ye say, lass,” he says, “But I’ll be thinkin' ay ye.”

As if he still doesn’t understand, he surprises me with a peck on my cheek. He looks at me in the eyes as I’m trying not to cry, and then he turns and exits the door, closing it tightly behind him.

I press my fingers to my cheek where his lips just touched. It’s warmer than usual and I can’t tell if that’s because of his kiss or my growing frustration.

five

I NEED TO LEAVE. I can't work with Roban and his crew working outside my dining room window, not after what transpired this evening. Not knowing where else to go, and not being able to afford a vacation, I decide to call my mother.

"Mom?" I say after she picks up the receiver.

"Emily? What is it? Are you all right?"

"Yes," I lie, "Why wouldn't I be?"

I forget that all she does is worry about me, especially after I left David. She thinks I am incapable of taking care of myself because I've always had someone there to do it for me, and maybe there's some truth to that, but I feel like I am doing better.

"You only call when there's something wrong. It's only natural that I would assume you are distressed," she says.

"That's not true," I say, "We talk all the time."

"Not as frequently as I would like. Tell me, what's going on?"

She knows me too well. It almost makes me feel bad for not calling her more than once a month.

"Mom, can I come stay with you for a little bit?"

"Of course, honey. When should I expect you?"

Just like that, she doesn't press the issue any further and I think that our relationship is less strained than I figured.

"I can be there tomorrow morning around... Oh, I don't know. If I leave by seven, I can be there by ten o'clock?"

"I'll be waiting for you. Drive safely! Don't speed through the canyon. Just because there isn't snow this time of year doesn't mean that you can't crash," she says.

"Mom, do you want me to come or not?"

"Okay, okay," she says, "I'll see you tomorrow."

We hang up the phone without saying goodbye, as we always do. There's something so final about goodbyes that makes us both uncomfortable. Probably because neither of us expected our farewells to my father to be our last. Ever since he passed, we always left our conversations hanging there, waiting to be picked up again at a later date.

I start packing my things and ask Alice if she will watch Vanta while I'm gone. Between a bag containing enough clothes for a week and my art supplies, and of course the giant canvas that I had sketched on earlier, there was barely enough room in my car for myself. I have to move the seat as forward as I possibly can to fit the canvas in the hatchback with the backseats down.

It's two hundred and thirty two miles to Moab where my mother lives, a three to four hour drive. I'm awake by six o'clock, and with my car already loaded from the night before, I am on the road with a travel mug full of coffee by seven, as promised.

I navigate my way to the highway before merging off in Spanish Fork to trek through the canyon, my car struggling to slowly ascend Soldier's Summit. The drive is beautiful, displaying everything that keeps me living in Utah: winding roads through forests of rich green pine trees with traces of snow the closer I get to the summit, even in the height of summer; then, as I descend the mountain, I am always surprised by the transition to bright orange and red rock formations, with layers of white like frosting in a tiered desert cake. Once I see the famous Hole in the Rock station, I know I am getting close to Moab. An hour away, at most.

I never really understood why my mother chose to move from Salt Lake City to Moab. Maybe she needed to escape the memories of my father to save herself by starting new somewhere else, somewhere magnificent and peaceful. I don't blame her. If I weren't such a city girl myself, I would join her. Moab has always been great for inspiration, which is why I try to visit my mother as often as I can. But winters make the drive too dangerous and stressful, so I usually only bother during the summer.

In fact, it's been nearly a year since I last saw my mother, so I suppose a visit was due. It's just a shame that I have to spend all of my time working on the commission instead of catching up with her. Although, I forget how tiresome my mother can be. Even though I return to Moab every year, I always stay too long, as if I'll never see her again. Then she drives me nuts and I leave, telling myself I'll never come back. Then we talk on the phone and everything is fine. So, I return the next year and the next. And so the cycle continues.

Soon, Highway 191 turns into Main Street and I am comforted by the eclectic desert shops and restaurants. Main Street, for the most part, is lined with hotels and motels, as well, but I won't be staying at any of those. I'll be staying at my mother's house, in the guest bedroom which she will undoubtedly have prepared with perfectly clean, pressed sheets and enough throw pillows in which to drown myself.

I decide to pull up at the gas station to fill up. As the gasoline pump clicks and whirrs, I check my phone for the first time after the long drive. I have a missed call from Alice. Not too surprising, but a little worrisome. I wonder if something went wrong at the house. I take the pump out of the fuel filler and climb back into my car to escape the sound of heavy traffic on Main Street and dial Alice's number. She picks up after one ring.

"Alice, sorry I missed your call. I was driving. Is everything okay?"

I hear her giggle slightly, and at that, my heart stops pounding.

"Oh, everything is fine. I'm just working on my book and Vanta is off doing god knows what," she says. I can hear her lips curling with each syllable. She's holding something back.

"Then why did you call? You know I'll be gone for at least a week," I say curiously. My question is only met with more giggling.

"You'll never guess who came looking for you this morning," she teases.

"Who?" I ask. *Please don't say Roban. Please don't say Roban.*

"Just a certain handsome landscaper with a funny name and a charming accent. He left something for you. It's wrapped. Should I open it?"

Fuck. I let out a loud and deep sigh. "No, don't touch it. Did he say anything?"

"Sure he did. He was wondering where you were and I told him you were skipping town for a week or so. I gave him your mother's number. I hope you don't mind," she says.

"You *what?*"

"He asked how to get a hold of you and—"

"Alice! I left town to *get away* from Roban. I can't deal with him calling me while I am trying to work." I don't mean to snap at Alice, but how can she be so careless? Her incessant goading since she first saw Roban in our yard has been irritating to say the least. She doesn't approve of my decision not to date after my divorce. Well, she hasn't said as much, but it shows every time she tries to swoop in and push me toward other men.

"Sorry, I didn't know that. I just thought you could benefit from a little human connection—besides me, of course. I don't count," she says before pausing for my reaction, but my head is starting to ache and I don't know what to say. "Emily, listen. You have been too withdrawn since you left David. I know the divorce was hard, but you need to put yourself back out there. There is someone out there that could truly love you if you gave them the chance. Why not Roban? He's clearly obsessed with you and he isn't half bad to look at. You could do a lot worse."

"You're missing the point," I say, rubbing my temples with my hand, "I don't *want* to be with anyone *ever*. I just want to focus on my art, get into a gallery, and learn how to be self sufficient. I haven't had the space to be myself in more than ten years, Alice. Now I finally have the freedom to create the life that I want, and I'm not going to throw that away over a handsome Scottish dude that recites poetry and has a man-bun."

The other line is silent. I imagine there's not much to say to that. I put my foot down. I said my peace.

"Emily, I think *you're* missing the point. Falling in love

—real love, not whatever fucked up thing you had with David was—doesn't mean sacrificing yourself or your independence."

"And what makes you think that Roban is the right guy?"

"He told me what happened between you two yesterday. The way he talks about you is so wholesome. Despite how rude you were, he still wants to be with you. Isn't that worth something?"

I can feel myself getting emotional again. I had replayed the events of yesterday in my head the entire drive from Salt Lake City to Moab. I couldn't get him out of my head, despite my better judgement. I dab my eyes with the collar of my t-shirt and compose myself.

"No, it's not. Now look, I have to go. Don't call me unless the house is on fire," I joke.

Alice laughs and says goodbye. I hang up and hide my phone in the center console of my car. No more distractions. I put the car in drive and travel the remaining couple of blocks to my mother's house.

When I pull up, it looks exactly the same as the last time I was here. The house has beige vinyl paneling with vibrant red accents around the doors and windows. After all, red is my mother's favorite color. There is no lawn—why would there be in a desert?—just decorative rocks of various sizes and lots of colorful ornaments sticking out of the ground. It seems like she's added more since I was here last.

My mother greets me at the door and helps me unload the car, which I greatly appreciate since I packed so much. She has always been a helpful host. It's just when she starts lecturing me that I get fed up, say something I regret, and leave for home earlier than I had planned. But I hope this trip will be different. Since I plan to spend so much of my time painting, I believe that we will give each other the space we need to be pleasant to one another.

I set up the canvas on her back patio, which is shaded and surrounded with potted succulents. Normally, I would just lay down an old sheet over the carpet in the guest room and paint there, but with a canvas this size, I worried that it wouldn't fit. Fortunately, the desert air is dry and, in the shade at least, the temperature isn't too sweltering. Especially if I paint during the evenings when a strange chill settles over the towering red-rock plateaus and the valley below.

After I've unpacked, my mother offers me a cold beer from a local brewery, which I gladly accept having worked up a sweat in the heat. Summers aren't the best time to visit Moab. During the day, it gets dangerously hot, and if you don't stay hydrated, you could easily escalate to a heat stroke. But I needed to get away. I need to focus on this painting so I can pay my bills. It's a matter of survival.

My mother and I sit in silence as we drink beer and watch TV. After a while, my mom clears her throat. "So, Emily," she begins.

"Yes?" I say, taking a swig of my beer.

"I don't know how to tell you this, so I'll just say it. Emily, I've been seeing someone."

I nearly choke on my beer. "Excuse me?"

"I'm seeing someone," she repeats. "Have been for quite a few months now."

My veins feel like they're on fire. "You've been dating someone for *months* and you are just telling me now? What the fuck, Mom?"

"Language," she scolds. "And yes. His name is Robert and--"

"What about Dad? Did he mean nothing to you?" My words are catching in my throat.

"Your father died more than a decade ago, Emily. I've grieved long enough. I'm happy now," she says, a softness in her stare that challenges my anger head-on. "Don't you want me to be happy?

"Of course I want you to be happy," I say, "But I thought you already were."

She rubs her temples aggressively. "I was happy, or so I thought. But I realized I'd been missing something."

"And what's that?"

"Companionship," she says. "Robert has been a true friend to me for many years, ever since I moved to Moab. I don't know how to explain it, but we fell for each other, Emily. These things happen. This is a good thing."

I won't hear it. I clam up and suddenly, I have nothing to say. I am furious, naturally. It all feels like a betrayal to Dad, even if he is long deceased. My parents were in love. Not everyone can say that, but my parents were head over heels in love. How can she just get over that?

My mind is itching to check my phone, which I had turned off after my call with Alice. As much as I hate to admit it, I am addicted to social media as much as any other millennial. I crave it during empty moments when nothing else is grabbing my attention.

I reach in my pocket and withdraw my phone. I stare at it, debating whether I really want to turn it on. Ultimately, my curiosity gets the better of me and I hold down the power button until all of my apps appear on the screen. It takes a minute or two to detect a signal. Even though Moab is filled with tourists, it's a small town located in the middle of nowhere. The one bar of cell service that I get reminds me of that fact.

As soon as it connects, my phone vibrates. A voicemail notification appears on the screen. I check it only to discover that I missed a call from Roban.

I press the phone to my ear and hold my breath as I listen to his message.

"Emily, It's me. Roban. Ah hope ye don't min' me callin'. You gae me yer number sae Ah figured Ah woods call. Ah brooght ye somethin'. Ah don't ken if Alice tauld ye 'at. Ah guess yoo'll jist hae tae open it when ye gie back. Anyway, th' reason Ah cam tae th' hoose an' th' reason I'm callin' ye noo is coz Ah ken ye got scared yesterday. But Ah want ye tae gife me a chance. We can tak' it slaw. Call me back an' lit me ken if yoo'll humur me wi' jist one date. Ah hope tae see ye suin. Tak' caur, lass."

I sniff and text the number back, "Not a chance."

But I can't help but feel like I am making the wrong decision.

six

IT'S early morning and I am on my mother's patio as the sun crests over the red rock plateaus, casting a ginger glow over the desert below. As I sip my coffee, I continue working on the Conway painting. I should be focused. After all, why else did I drive down here?

But I can't get Roban's voicemail out of my mind. I want to know what gift he brought me. I want to know what he expects of me. I want to know what it's like to lay my head on his broad shoulders and run my fingers through the hair on his chest. *No. Stop that.* I can't. I need to focus.

I tap my brush onto my paint palette and begin making small strokes. I think about what Roban said about the signs that Margaret and Charles are clearly in love. I need to emphasize these details with my brush: the creases of their happy, squinting eyes; Charles's arm around Margaret's waist; the minimal distance between them. Yet I feel like I'm missing something, the intangible spark as Roban called it, as I paint their portrait. I'm so engrossed by my work that I hardly notice the afternoon wave of heat scorching the earth beyond the patio canopies. I keep painting until my brain exhausts itself before going inside and leaving the paint to dry.

"I see you're making good progress out there," my mother says as she pours herself a glass of iced tea. "Tea?"

I dab the sweat from my forehead with my raggedy, old, paint-stained shirt, getting a little bit of phthalo blue on my brow. "Yes," I say, "That sounds perfect."

My mother hands me a large glass brimming with ice and sweet tea, condensation already dripping off the sides. I drink it eagerly, quickly consuming all of the tea until all I am left with is a glass of half-melted ice. I help myself to some more. Water would probably be preferable since I forgot to stay hydrated while I was painting outside, but the sweet tea is so much more refreshing.

I sit at the counter while my mother prepares a nice, cool dinner. She's vegan now, has been since she moved to Moab, so she's always making salads. Tonight is no exception. I watch as she carefully removes kale from its stems, cutting the leaves into smaller pieces. But her hand is shaking violently as she cuts. I fear for her fingers. She tosses the kale in a bowl.

"Mom?"

"Yes, dear."

"Why are you shaking like that?" I ask.

Her mouth twists and she sets the knife in the sink, trembling all the while. "Must be nerves, I suppose."

"Have you seen a doctor?"

"No," she says, avoiding my concerned gaze. "That won't be necessary."

"Mom, you really need to get that checked. Maybe it's nerves, but what if it's something worse?"

"Fine. I'll make an appointment with my doctor. Happy?"

I am pleased to hear it, but it's all still very alarming.

I get lost in my own thoughts. Mostly, I feel bad about my text to Roban yesterday. Part of me wants to text him back, tell him I'm sorry, and tell him I'd love to go on a date with him. But I know I get too distracted when he is near, and I don't want him to derail the plans I have for my future. For the first time in ten years, I actually feel like I have a future and that I control my destiny. Dating would only complicate things, take away the freedom I didn't know I had so thoroughly missed.

"Everything okay, Emily?" my mother says, looking up from the cutting board. She's stopped chopping. I didn't even notice.

My eyes meet hers and I don't know why, but I get this feeling that I might cry. I drop my head and pull at my hair, groaning in agony. "Ugh, no. I feel stuck," I say.

My mother goes back to preparing the kale salad. "With your painting? It seems like it's going fine. Just keep going—"

"No," I say, "Not with the painting. With my life."

"What about it?" she asks, "You're only thirty-three. You've got your whole life ahead of you."

"It doesn't feel that way," I moan. "It's just... I'm trying so hard to succeed as an artist and get my work into a posh gallery. It's more than a full-time job just trying to catch up on commissions so I can pay my bills while also working on my own creative projects. It's exhausting."

"Emily, you've been painting your whole life. You've already achieved so much as an artist. Don't discount your current success. Think about where you've been and where you are now. Don't worry so much about the future."

It's good advice, but it doesn't make me feel any better. "Yeah, I guess," I say.

I feel my mother's eyes scrutinizing me. "There's something else, isn't there?"

Damn her for knowing me so well.

"How can you tell?" I ask, curious whether my mother has taken up witchcraft. What else could explain her impeccable intuition?

She shakes her head, chuckling to herself, "You don't normally get so anxious about painting. But I understand your fears for the future. You've never experienced the freedom of being alone. Someone's always had to take care of you, and now you are taking care of yourself and it's empowering. I know because I felt the same way after your father died. Not immediately, but over time, it became easier. So tell me, what's really on your mind?"

I let out a deep sigh. "There's this guy," I admit.

"I knew it!" my mother exclaims. "Sorry, continue."

I begin picking at my cuticles. "Anyway, he's interested in me, and I think I'm interested in him, but I hate the way I feel. My heart is always pounding, my veins feel like they're on fire, and I can't sleep. He seems like a decent enough guy, but like you said, someone's always taken care of me and I *am* enjoying my independence. I'm afraid that if I fall for someone again, I'll lose myself entirely."

My mother clicks her tongue at me. "So things didn't work out with David. Big deal. I told you as much when you said you were getting married. Now your life really begins, and if you don't want to live that life alone, I suggest you start dating again."

"Mother!" I shout as she massages the kale in an olive oil dressing.

"What? It's true. If you like this guy, then just go for it. You don't want to be living life twenty years later wondering what could have been. What's the worst that can happen?" She pauses and I can tell both of our minds conjure David. "Okay, so the worst has already happened. Unless you mean to tell me you learned nothing from your divorce, it's not bound to happen again."

I sigh and rub my forehead with the tips of my fingers. "Mom, it's like you haven't been listening. Didn't you feel like you lost a part of yourself when you married Dad?"

"No," she says frankly, "No, I think I grew as a person when we were together. That's how you know the love is real. They won't hold you back. They'll support you and help you become the best version of yourself that you can possibly be. I know you didn't have that with David. That's clear enough for anyone to see. But that wasn't love, sweetheart. That was codependence. That was toxic. That was a sham, if I'm being honest with you. And now you are relishing in your freedom, and I support that. But maybe this new guy can help you discover an entirely new kind of freedom, one in which you become a better artist and a better person. You'll never know unless you try."

She dishes a heaping pile of southwestern kale salad onto a plate and hands it to me. I understand what she is trying to tell me, but I don't want to hear it. She asked what's the worst that could happen. She and I both know how bad it can be. Maybe it could be even worse, for all I know.

I'll admit, I'm not that experienced when it comes to love. I was too weird in high school, so no one ever saw me as a viable romantic partner. I never had a boyfriend then, even though I kissed my best friend, William, regularly. He wanted to preserve our friendship, but fast forward sixteen years and our friendship was ruined anyway. Probably from all the aforementioned kissing.

I was twenty-one when I first met David. My father had

just died and I needed to see a psychiatrist to cope. That psychiatrist was David. The first thing he did was diagnose me with bipolar disorder, generalized anxiety disorder, major depression, and to my surprise, an eating disorder, as well. I was a mess, desperate for help wherever I could find it. David helped me for a few months, offering counseling and adjusting my medications, until one day he called me in an... unprofessional manner. I was so broken that I rushed to his bed, and I confused the trust I had placed in him and my health with love.

What I lost during those ten years is unspeakable. Once I slept with David, I found a new psychiatrist to help me balance my mood, but David still held this power over me. There were things I wasn't allowed to do, like cut my hair short, listen to pop music, or hang out with my friends. However, since he offered to support my career as an artist, I confused his intense personality and his rules as loving protection. Little did I know that I was being abused all along.

I didn't speak of these things to my new psychiatrist. It felt like a betrayal to David, and after all he did to help my art, I couldn't speak of the discomfort I felt and that seemed to only deepen my sadness. I repressed the thoughts I had that something was wrong. And all throughout our relationship, I lost myself entirely. The only thing I was allowed to be was wife and artist, and wife always seemed to come first.

I eat my salad slowly, reflecting on the last few months following the divorce, remembering how I felt these last eleven years. I'm not sure whether it is worth the risk, but something urges me to reach out to Roban and apologize for my behavior. My reluctance comes from a place of fear, I know this. But it protects me from trapping myself in another abusive relationship.

I lose concentration and suddenly chewing is more work than it's worth. I need to contact Roban. I need to explain.

"Excuse me," I say hastily, grabbing my cell phone off of the kitchen counter and exiting the sliding glass door leading to the patio.

I decide to work more on the Conway painting so I can mull things over lest I do something regretful. With each brush stroke, I feel like I am getting closer to being finished, but I am still missing the emotion needed to sustain the portrait. I suppose there are still many brush strokes I haven't made yet. Ones that live in my bones but I haven't been able to execute.

I squeeze more raw sienna and yellow ochre onto my palette and mix them with a bit of the white that already rests beside them. I begin painting faster and faster until the light outside extinguishes and I exhaust myself. I go back inside and collapse upon the guest bed, staring at my phone in my hand. Before I know it, I'm dialing Roban's number.

The phone rings several times and for what feels like an eternity, I'm not sure that he will pick up. It is late, after all. Just after ten o'clock at night. Then, I hear a click, a loud crashing noise, and a muffled "*Shit,*" on the other line.

"Sorry, hi. Drapped mah phone." he says.

"Hi, Roban. It's Emily," I say.

A light chuckle. "Ah ken. I'm surprised ye called efter Ah got 'at text frae ye yesterday."

My cheeks feel flushed and I become acutely aware of how warm it is in my mother's guest room. I take a deep breath. There is so much I want to say but don't know how to articulate. "Sorry, I know it's late. And sorry about the text, too. That was rude. I don't know what came over me."

"It's braw," he says, "Whit can Ah dae fur ye?"

"I umm...," I pause for a minute. "I just wanted an update on the yard."

Silence on the other end. "Ye called me in th' middle ay th' nicht fur an update oan yer yard?"

"Yep," I say, a little frazzled. "Just curious if you'd done the rock yet."

"Yes," Roban says, drawing out his vowels as if he is confused. He is confused, no doubt. I think we both know I don't really care about the yard right now. "Th' rock was drapped aff thes morn. It took a coople ay hoors, but we got it aw laid it an' graded. We jist need tae plant th' yuccas, th' butterfly bushes, an' a new chokecherry tree, but 'at has tae bide until yer order at th' nursery comes in next week."

"Next week," I repeat, "That's good. And then I suppose you'll be done then?"

"That's reit."

Silence.

"Well, I guess I should let you go. Thank you for the update," I say, very professionally I might add.

"Emily, when ur ye comin' back?" he pleads.

There's pain in his voice, and it makes me feel terrible that I ever left.

"Soon," I say, "I'm almost done with the portrait." But I realize he doesn't care about all that. At least, if he does, he doesn't let on. "Listen, I'd like to see you when I'm back."

"I'd loch 'at," he says.

"Great," I mumble, "Well, I have to go. I'll see you soon, okay?"

"I'm lookin' forward tae it, lass."

I hang up and slap the phone against my forehead

repeatedly. *Stupid, stupid, stupid.* At least he was amicable. I'm not sure I would have been after receiving my text.

Hearing his voice cleared my head a little bit, or are things more fuzzy? I can't tell. All I know is that I feel something for him, and if my mother is right, it might be worth the risk.

I rest my head on my pillow, which is warm and damp from the sweat on my neck. As I drift off to sleep, all I can see is Roban's stupidly handsome face. I fight off the visions, but he keeps returning to me, his dark beard wrapped around his perfect smile, pieces of hair falling over his eyes. My heart lightens, yet it beats furiously at the same time. I think I'm hopeful about him, but a little scared. I don't know what I'll say to him when I return to Salt Lake City, but I'm sure I'll find the words. Eventually.

For now, I sleep. Tomorrow, I will rise early and get to work on Margaret's portrait. It should take a couple more days at most. I haven't lost sight of why I came to Moab. I need to finish. I need to get paid. I need to pay my mortgage. And then, maybe after that, I'll have room in my life for Roban.

seven

IT TAKES me five whole days to finish the Conway painting. I can't wait to show Roban, though I try to contain my excitement. I think it's the best work I've ever done. I hope I captured the intangible spark, but it's difficult for me to tell without having seen it or experienced it myself. I suppose my parents had that spark. You wouldn't be able to tell if you saw my mother now, but she loved my father fiercely. It's possible that their love gave me false hope that I would love someone else just as much. Those hopes were dashed a couple years into my marriage, but what could I do? David supported me and I couldn't survive without him.

Now I'm feeling cautiously optimistic. True, I don't know Roban that well, but there's something about him that is so undeniably tender. I don't believe he could hurt me, and that notion gives me power, like my heart is invincible.

I begin packing up my car as my mother sips tea on the front porch.

"Are you sure you don't need any help?" she calls. I'm

carefully creating a soft base on which to set the giant canvas in the back of my car. She means well, but I want to do this on my own. Only I know how to arrange my belongings in a way that won't compromise the Conway painting. If anything happened to it, I would be utterly screwed.

"Yes, Mom. I got this. Go inside, it's too hot out," I say.

She doesn't listen. I imagine she's more accustomed to this climate than I am anyway. *She can take care of herself,* I remind myself. I sincerely believe it, too, even if, admittedly, her tremors have me greatly concerned. However, if my mom could learn how to be happy and self-sufficient after my father died, then I could move on from my divorce and build the future I want for myself. I believe this, too. The phoenix must rise again. I have to, or else I would just crumble into a pile of ashes.

After gently setting the painting down on top of the padded base I created, I slam the trunk closed and give my mother a big hug.

"Good luck with your art, and good luck with this mystery man of yours," she says, cracking a smile.

My cheeks bloom and I look down sheepishly. "Thanks, Mom."

"And don't wait so long to visit next time, okay? I'm only three hours away."

"Yes, Mom," I say. I kiss my mother on the cheek and walk towards my car. "Love you!"

She says she loves me back and goes back inside where it's cool as I pull out of the driveway. It's weird: I always felt uneasy telling David I loved him, probably because I knew it wasn't true. But how naturally I can say it to my mother astounds me. As I drive through the canyons, ascending the mountain roads, I realize that my unconditional love for my mother is proof that I am capable of loving another person.

I just haven't found the *right* person. Someone I could truly call family.

It's too soon to say whether Roban is that person, but I feel like he has the potential. His intimacy with the earth keeps him grounded, and perhaps his Scottish heritage is what makes him appreciate the beauty of the little things, as evidenced by his love of poetry. But that's all I really know about him, so I'm afraid of being disappointed. There has to be a catch, right? Maybe he's a complete and utter asshole deep down, but I'm willing to excavate his personality to find out.

There were plenty of red flags to tell me who David was at his core. He was my psychiatrist, for starters. In retrospect, I really should have noted the power imbalance. There was the fact he was significantly older, as well, which should have indicated to me that I was being groomed. After all, I was not much older than a teenager. Then there was the fact that he was married when we met. He left his wife to be with me, and there is no surer sign that a person will be unfaithful than if your relationship grew from infidelity.

David was always on his phone. Texting patients, he would say. But knowing what I knew about his intimacy with patients, I should have been more suspicious. My ex-husband kept many secrets from me, I'm sure. Not just the affair. The affair was just one unfortunate discovery, though it woke me up from my nightmare and provided an exit from his emotional abuse. A normal wife would be devastated, but I was just... happy. I felt real, genuine joy for the first time in more than ten years.

I would be vigilant now. If I were going to put my trust in Roban, I would need to get to know him slowly, learning everything I could about him until there was no room for secrets. I'd need reassurance that we were on equal footing. That means splitting dates fifty-fifty, no huge discrepancies in income, no dependency on one another. I would need ample space to work on my art and he would need to understand that is where my priorities lie. I wouldn't want to be his priority either. I'd need to know that he has a rich inner life that doesn't require my presence to fill a void.

I have so many conditions for dating Roban that I wonder if I am taking it too far. But then I remember that my lack of boundaries is what ultimately led to my failed marriage with David, and I refuse to go through all of that again. I refuse to be the victim of another abusive relationship, though I understand how it can happen to women over and over again.

During my drawn-out divorce, I searched the internet for answers. Why had I put up with as much as I had with David? It's confusing and heartbreaking to realize I could have left at any time, but I needed to understand why I stayed. More importantly, after months of blaming myself, I needed to learn that it wasn't my fault.

Turns out, it's completely normal for a victim of abuse to move from one abusive relationship to another. This is one of the many reasons why I am so reluctant to get involved with Roban. I also learned that I can't trust my instincts, as so many red flags went undetected with David. I would need to go into a new relationship with my guard up, possibly for a long time, and I'd need to rely on the opinions of my friends and family to assess the risks. Alice would be good for this, I decide, since she is already acquainted with Roban and is just as jaded when it comes to love as I am. I take the fact that she is pushing me to date our landscaper as a good sign.

It takes me hours to get out of the canyon and back into

the valley. Once I pass through Provo, I am speeding down the highway, aching for home. But I know I need to make a stop at the post office before I can curl up on the couch in my bungalow. Margaret will be expecting her painting and I will be expecting a fat check.

Fortunately, the post office is down the street from the bungalow. The postal worker at the counter helps me fit it safely and snugly into a large, skinny box. We put styrofoam corners on the edges of the canvas before slipping it inside, filling the empty space with bubble wrap. They slap a shipping label on it, and before I know it, I am out the door and on my way back home.

The door is unlocked, which Alice always does when she is home, driving me crazy. However, I am relieved when I walk in to find her typing away at her laptop while she is reclined on the couch. At least she didn't stray too far from the door.

"Working on your book?" I ask as I set my bags down on the floor.

"Yeah, what else is new?" she says, her voice brimming with sarcasm. "I didn't know you'd be back today. But I'm glad you're here. Now, will you please open Roban's gift? I am dying to know what's inside!"

Alice points to the coffee table where a small decorative bag with wisps of crepe paper sticking out of the top sits, waiting for me. She leans forward as I peek inside, gently tugging the crepe paper out of the bag. Inside, I see an array of new paint brushes with a folded note attached to them. I pluck the note from the bag and read it aloud so Alice can hear. I realize immediately that it is part of a poem handwritten in immaculate cursive:

Were I in the wildest waste,
Sae black and bare, sae black and bare,

The desert were a Paradise,
If thou wert there, if thou wert there.

I recognize it as the line from the Robert Burns poem that Roban had quoted when we were analyzing Margaret Conway's photograph. My heart swells at the gesture, but then I catch myself having feelings, so I squash them down. *Careful, Emily. Careful.*

"He wrote you a poem?" Alice squeals in delight. She's clearly more excited about it than I am.

"No," I correct her, "He's quoting Robert Burns. He recited a line of it to me before we almost..." I trail off. Alice doesn't need me to finish the thought. It's like she already knows.

"Well, even if he didn't write it, what man in this century tries to woo a woman with poetry? Take the gesture for what it is: he *likes* you, Emily. I know I'm normally a cynic about this sort of thing, but really, you should give him a chance."

She doesn't need to tell me. I'm more cynical than she is and I still couldn't get Roban off my mind the entire time I was in Moab.

I'll admit I was anxious about the gift. I wasn't sure if it would be something sappy like a mixtape or a bunch of flowers. I'm relieved to find the brushes instead. I caress the bristles and admire the handles of each one. Rather than being made of wood, they appear to be made of a translucent orange resin or something. The orange is bright and cheerful, just like the curtains in my painting room. He must have seen them when I invited him inside.

"I'm going to text him right now, I promise," I say to Alice, but also a bit to myself.

"You're going to text him? Real romantic, Emily," Alice jokes.

"Just to get his address," I say, "And shut up! I'm not trying to be romantic. I just want to see where this goes."

Roban answers my text immediately, reluctantly noting his address. Although I'm tired from the long drive back to Salt Lake City, it's only just early evening, so there is plenty of time to drive to the other side of the valley to visit Roban. I need to get things off my chest, things that haunted me during my entire visit with my mother.

It takes no more than twenty minutes to get to Roban's house. The house is small, with red brick and metal handrails and cracked cement steps leading up to the wooden door. I ascend the steps, nearly falling off as the handrails sway out of place. I'm alarmed that his house is in such a state of disrepair. I knock on the door gently, but no one answers. I decide I must be more forceful, or perhaps I should just leave altogether. As I wrestle with my indecision, I see the blinds move in the front window, and then, almost instantly, the door swings open.

An unfamiliar man stands in the doorway. I've never seen him before. He's tall and lanky with blonde hair, wearing a dirty t-shirt and some grease-stained sweatpants.

"Can I help you?" he asks. He seems annoyed, like I've just interrupted him doing something. It dawns on me that maybe I'm at the wrong address.

"Hi, umm... Does Roban live here? Roban Campbell?"

"Who's asking?" he says icily.

Suddenly, I hear loud steps behind the skinny blonde man. Roban appears behind him, setting his hand firmly on his shoulder.

"Sorry, lass. Thes is Matt, mah hoosemate. He's friendlier than he lets oan, Ah promise," he says cheerfully.

Matt grunts disapprovingly. I extend my hand to shake

his, but he rolls his eyes and disappears behind the doorway where Roban and I are standing.

"He hates me," I say.

"Nae," Roban says, "Not hate. Nae hate. Yoo'll hae tae forgife his manners. He's jist nae much ay a people person."

We stand there awkwardly for a long minute before Roban invites me inside. It's a typical bachelor pad. Nothing matches, but either Roban or Matt have splurged on the necessities: a large flatscreen TV mounted to the wall, every video game console I know of, and an enormous, garnet suede L-section couch in the center of the room. Roban invites me to sit on the couch, which I do warily. The interaction with his housemate, Matt, has me second-guessing myself.

"Sae, whit did ye come aw thes way fur?" Roban asks.

I twist my hair in my fingers and look down at my feet. "Right," I say, "I just wanted to thank you for the paint brushes. They are beautiful and that was a really thoughtful gift."

"Nae worries, mah sister actually—" he says, but I'm feeling bolder by the second and I have to get the words out.

"I'd like to go on a date with you," I say matter of factly.

Roban pauses and then his lips curl into a lopsided smile. It's quite endearing the longer I look at it. "Rilly?" he says in disbelief.

"Yes," I say, "But I have conditions."

Roban's smile disappears and his face sobers.

"I just went through a divorce, so I need to take things slow. I'll need lots of space—no clingyness, no codependence. I want to split everything fifty-fifty, and I don't want to get involved until my yard is finished. I just can't let you have anything to lord over me," I say, blurting out the words faster than I can process them. I've rehearsed this in my head a million times over the last few days, but it's not coming out as eloquently as I had hoped. Still, Roban nods and his eyes are studying me, taking in every messy word I say. "And my art needs to come first. You understand, right?"

"Aye," he says, surprising even me, "Ah promise Ah will respect yer space an' Ah won't come atween ye an' yer art. Ah think Ah micht hae mentioned thes before, but Ah am recoverin' frae a relationship myself. Before Ah moved haur months ago, Ah was engaged tae mah college sweetheart. But she got col' feit an' broke aff uir engagement. Wanted tae experience mair ay life before she settled doon, fur which Ah can hardly blam 'er. Still, it hurt. Bad. I'm a broken man, lass. But Ah wooldn't be sae persistent if Ah didn't hae a guid feelin' abit ye."

I am dumbstruck. I know he had mentioned a terminated engagement before, but I hadn't given it much thought. It explains a lot the more I think about it. Unlike me, he is a hopeless romantic. He's truly loved and lost—and me, well, I've just lost. This makes me feel bad for him, like he's still grieving, so I set my hand lightly on his knee and stare into his eyes.

"I have a good feeling about you, too."

eight

I'M WAITING on my porch with my purse slung over my shoulder. Roban, who kindly agreed to pick me up for our first date, should arrive soon. My heart is racing and my breath is quicker than usual. I feel like I just sprinted up a huge flight of stairs even though I've just been sitting on the porch swing, anxiously swaying myself back and forth.

Alice is waiting with me, sitting on one of the Adirondack chairs while she laughs at my inability to sit still. I shoot her a menacing look as she makes fun of my situation.

"It will be fine. Just take deep breaths. You don't want to faint on your first date—or do you?" Alice chuckles. "Oh, I know! Pretend to faint and he'll scoop you up into his big arms!"

"What is this? A regency novel?" I joke.

"I wouldn't know," Alice says, "I only read nonfiction."

"What happens in your nonfiction books?"

"Oh, I don't know. I suppose the woman usually gets murdered," she says.

I sigh and cup my head into my hands. "Great, thanks. That's a relief."

At this point, our date has been built up in not just Alice's mind, but my mind, as well. It doesn't help that Roban refuses to tell me where he's taking me. I told him if he's planning on taking me to a fancy restaurant, I need to know so I can dress the part (not that I have anything that isn't covered in paint). He told me to just dress like myself, so I put on my cleanest pair of overall shorts and a vibrant, multicolored, striped blouse. If we were going to be outside, I wanted to be prepared so I wouldn't melt like a popsicle.

"I'm just messing with you," Alice says, swirling a glass of chardonnay in one hand. "Roban doesn't seem like the murdering type."

"That's because murderers never do," I snap.

Our conversation is interrupted by a loud roar, so loud that the ground rumbles below our feet. A black motorcycle with an empty back seat pulls up to the curb. I can tell the man parking the motorcycle with the plaid shirt and the stocky build is Roban before he even removes his helmet.

"You've got to be kidding," Alice says as Roban turns off the engine.

He approaches the porch with the helmet in one hand, keys in the other, his arms outstretched like peacock feathers.

"No, no, no, no, no," I say, "I am *not* getting on that thing," I shout, which is unnecessary, but I am deathly terrified of motorcycles. I've only been on one once with my dad, and he accelerated so quickly that I fell off the back and nearly broke my back when I flew back onto the asphalt. Ever since then, I have refused to ride on one again, even if it's a handsome man trying to take me out on a date.

"What's wrang? It's safe," Roban coos, stuffing the keys into the pocket of his jeans, "I'll e'en lit ye wear th' helmit."

"Absolutely not, I am not getting on that thing," I say, stomping my foot down.

Alice is snickering behind me, but I don't care. Riding on that thing is completely out of the question.

"He did come all this way to see you," Alice says, trying to contain her laughter.

"Aye, she's reit, lass. I'll drife real slaw. Uir date is jist near th' park," he says. He extends his arm toward me, beckoning me to take his hand. Before I know it, Alice is literally shoving my body forward. I trip as I try to resist, but Roban catches me by the hand and pulls me up to my feet, my figure inches away from his.

Roban smiles a crooked smile as he gently leads me toward the motorcycle, but I can feel my body trembling. We stand on the curb and Roban carefully pulls the helmet down onto my head, fastening its straps tightly so it doesn't wobble. I think he can tell how afraid I am. How could he not with my limbs shuddering like this? He holds me still by the shoulders and looks me in the eye.

"It will be okay, Ah promise," he says. There's something in the sincerity of his face that makes me believe him. I take a deep breath.

"Okay," I say, and I hold his hand again, rough and warm against my palm, as he helps me straddle the back seat.

"Keep yer feit whaur they ur. Don't lit them tooch th' pipe reit thaur, ur else it will burn ye. An' when Ah lean, ye lean wi' me. Got it?" he says, far too quickly if I might add, because the words go in one ear and out the other and I realize I don't comprehend the important things he is telling me. Fortunately there is a back piece to my seat, so when the motorcycle lurches forward, I don't fall off.

I wrap my arms around Roban's sturdy frame as he very slowly, and very cautiously, navigates the bustling streets of Sugar House and then Liberty Wells near the park to which he is taking me. My legs are shaking, but I doubt he can feel it over the vibrations of the motorcycle's engine. I can't believe I am doing this.

Part of me wants to close my eyes and pretend I am somewhere else, but a larger part of me doesn't dare close my eyes for even a second. If this is how I die, I want to see it coming.

The trees whip past in a blur of green, and everything seems darker through the tinted visor of Roban's helmet. To keep my wits about me, I pay attention to the familiar houses that we pass along the way, all so cozy and unique. This gives me a little bit of comfort—that, and the strength of Roban's torso as I hold on for dear life.

I relax a little bit when we pull into the park. Roban drives especially slow as we go over the speed bumps. I see plenty of parking spaces, but he doesn't stop. He keeps creeping forward until we've nearly gone around the entire circumference of the park. At last, his secret is revealed to me when he finally pulls into a spot just outside the aviary.

He helps me out of the seat, guiding my legs so they don't touch the pipe that I barely remember him talking about. I struggle with the straps of the helmet, so, defeated, I kindly ask for Roban's assistance. I hate how this makes me feel. No autonomy. Completely at the mercy of Roban and his motorcycle. The whole experience has soured my mood, but I don't want to say anything because it might ruin the whole date. Still, Roban is too astute.

"Is everythin' okay?" he asks. Nothing goes past him, I swear.

"Yeah, just afraid of motorcycles," I confess, staring at the ground while I brush my hair behind my ear.

"Ye did great," he says. He gently lifts my chin and looks at me with tender eyes. "Rilly."

He takes hold of my hand, which I am grateful for as it helps me get my bearings as we walk toward the entrance to the aviary. Already, I can hear the squawking and calling of exotic birds. I haven't been to the aviary since I was a kid, so even if I did remember anything, surely it would have changed over the years.

Roban tries to pay for my admission, but I lower his hand holding his credit card and insist on paying my own way.

Roban respects my rules and pays only for his own ticket after letting me pay for mine first. Such a gentleman.

We walk into an open garden with winding paths leading to the various exhibits. I am struck by the beauty of it all.

"A lot has changed since I was last here," I say. "The gardens are new. So gorgeous!"

"Mah crew an' Ah jist designed an' planted everythin' in th' Sprin'. Glad tae hear ye loch it," Roban says shyly. His arms are folded across his chest as he looks at the ground, kicking around a pebble.

"You did all of *this*?" I ask, gesturing toward all of the trees and shrubs lining the paths.

"Aye," he says, "Weel, nae aw ay it. Most ay these trees waur awreddy haur. We mostly worked oan th' Children's Discovery Garden anyway. Ah can shaw ye if yoo'd loch?"

"Lead the way," I say, looping my hand through his

arm. He casts a smile downward, him standing so much taller than me. It's nice being close to someone like this.

We stop by every exhibit on the way to the garden, admiring everything from the colorful birds of the rain-forest to the many owls hiding on branches in the Owl Forest. We even take time to appreciate the common ducks, swans, and pelicans in the enormous pond.

"Ah used tae go birdin' wi' mah parents aw th' time when Ah was wee," Roban says as we approach the botanical garden. "When Ah foond it thaur was an aviary haur, Ah cooldn't bide tae brin' someain alang. but Ah guess things ne'er felt reit."

"Why is that?" I prod. I'm genuinely curious to know if this seemingly perfect man has as much baggage as I do.

"Efter Sophie, Ah was jist tay shy tae gab tae women. Was afraid ay bein' rejected."

"You? Shy?" I gasp. "You came onto me stronger than a cup of coffee."

Roban chuckles. I love that I can make him laugh. "Ah only pursued ye coz ye started screamin' at me ower 'at sick tree ay yoors. Ye rejected me before Ah e'en got an opportunity tae hae an opinion abit ye. In truth, Ah hated yer guts at th' start."

"What changed?" I ask.

"Ye cared enaw tae apologize," he says, stopping by the coral bells in the crevice garden. "Most Americans I've mit ur tay prood tae dae 'at. Most fowk don't caur at aw. Ye did though."

My cheeks flush. Rather than speaking, I pause to observe the other plants, like the arrowleaf balsamroot and fleabane. In the crevice garden, these plants have adapted to the harsh alpine landscapes. Because of the slabs of rock that lay like the pages of a book, they are sheltered and protected so the plants can thrive. The plants start out small, but over time, due to this nurturing environment that they have created, the plants get bigger and healthier until their flowers bloom.

"I've had a hard time controlling my temper," I explain, "Especially when other things are... well, out of my control."

Roban's chiseled, bearded face beams before me, urging me to look up at him. Reluctantly, I do.

"Fur whit it's worth, Ah was wrang abit ye," he says, "An' I'm pure glad ye apologized sae Ah coods gie tae ken th' real ye. If Ah waur a better man, Ah woods hae apologized first."

I can feel my cheeks burn, and I want to look away but I can't. Roban's eyes, blue as glaciers, are looking at me with such curiosity, such tenderness that I am immobilized by what I am feeling. My palms sweat and my heart beats faster. I want him to say another word, to break the silence that has held us for so long, but instead his attention is stolen by the loud ringing of his cell phone. It's volume is so high that I think it upsets the birds. At least, it has upset me.

Roban takes his phone out of his pocket and glances at the screen. I think I see a woman's name, but he moves the phone too quickly.

"Sorry, Ah hae tae tak' thes," he says, stepping away to a bench surrounded by peacocks.

I watch as he holds the phone up to his ear. He seems happy to be talking to whoever is calling him, smiling and laughing more than he does with me. *It's probably nothing*, I think to myself. I try to calm myself and think logically about this, but my mind is transported to my marital bedroom with a piece of silver jewelry rolling off the sheets. Roban is nothing like David, right?

I can feel my breathing getting ragged and suddenly I feel this urge to escape, but Roban appears at my side, and the touch of his hand on the small of my back brings me back to the present.

"Is everythin' okay?" he asks.

"Yeah," I lie, "I'm fine."

"Okay, guid, coz Ah want tae shaw ye somethin'!"

Roban takes my hand and pulls me along to the next exhibit: the sandhill cranes. They are tall and leggy, with gray bodies and crimson-capped heads. I don't know anything about this bird, and to me, it doesn't seem all that interesting. But Roban is very excited about it and his energy is contagious.

"Noo, thes bird was one Ah ne'er thooght Ah woods ever gie tae see," he says. "Growin' up in Oban, we didn't hae sandhill cranes. They can only be foond in wetlands an' prairies in North America."

"That's fascinating," I say, though it really isn't all that amusing. But I am enchanted by Roban's enthusiasm. He's so knowledgeable about everything, it seems.

"Yeah," he agrees, "Look at them dance!"

I watch the sandhill cranes in the enclosure. They stretch their wings, bob their heads, and leap into the air. It's very graceful.

"That's their coortship dance," Roban explains, "Efter their dance secures them a partner, they mate fur life. I've aye foond 'at bonnie."

I observe the cranes a bit longer until I see what Roban sees: two lovers entranced by each other, who find their partner and think, *We will be bonded for life.* Imagine such a thing. In my experience, not even humans can make that kind of commitment. Roban seems to think otherwise. I admire his optimism, and I wonder if he thinks I am his sandhill crane. Could he be mine? Maybe.

Watching the cranes dance with Roban's arm around me makes my heart swell. I've never felt more appreciated, more understood, than at this moment. In the distance, the sun is dipping below the mountains in the west. The sky erupts into a medley of colors, pinks and oranges blending into purples and blues like watercolor paint.

Roban turns me around so that I am facing him. I look up at him, his dark hair curled around his jawline, his bearded lips smooth and tempting. I stand on my tip toes and pull his face toward mine, drawing him into a deep kiss. One of his strong hands catches my waist while the other runs through my hair near the nape of my neck, gripping me softly but firmly. His lips are soft, as promised by the dappling golden light, and his mouth glides in sync with mine, devouring me hungrily as if I were a ripe, juicy peach.

Suddenly, I'm struck by inspiration. I want to go home and create an abstract painting that encapsulates this point in time. The sunset's divine palette and this feeling of warmth must be transferred to a canvas because I never want to forget it.

Instead, I take Roban home with me, still clinging to one another the whole ride back. I don't even mind the motorcycle.

nine

I WAKE up earlier than usual. It feels odd having someone other than David in my bed. It feels even odder having slept with someone other than him, too. *Eleven years.* We were together for eleven years. I had only had sex with one other person before David. And now, here lies Roban with nothing but a sheet draped over his groin. *Oh, it was so much fun though, wasn't it?*

Since the divorce, I've changed the sheets from bleach white to bright turquoise. Anything to liven up the bedroom, which was so minimalistic and modern before, like no one lived here at all. I crave personality for my space, and with that comes a complete makeover. I painted the headboard and the bedside tables a pale cadmium green in hopes that the room might resemble a jungle.

I've woken up in this newly designed room every day for months, but never has it glowed like the leaves in a treetop canopy like it is this morning, with Roban resting inside like he is Tarzan and I am Jane. It's just past dawn and the sun shimmers through the curtains, casting a delicate light on Roban's hairy chest as it rises and falls with each sleeping breath. I am captivated by him.

I think he senses me staring at him because after a long, silent moment, he blinks open his eyes, looks at me averting my gaze, and smiles with that devilish mouth of his. He reaches around me, his arms like thick branches enveloping me as he pulls me closer, resting my head on his chest. His breathing is different when he's awake. It's more vibrant and deliberate. And I've never noticed his scent before. He smells like rainy soil in a pine forest.

Roban kisses my head and says softly, "An I'll kiss thee yet, yet; An I'll kiss thee o'er again; An I'll kiss thee yet, yet; My bonnie Emily."

"Let me guess," I say, "More Robert Burns?"

"Am Ah 'at predictable?" he says, smoothing my hair behind my ear.

I chuckle and try to hide a smile. "I love when you recite poetry," I say, "You're flexing the sexiest muscle: that big brain of yours."

"Technically 'spikin, lass, th' brain isn't a muscle," he corrects me, "It's an organ, jist loch yer lungs ur yer heart."

"For a poet, you aren't very good at this whole dirty talking thing," I say as I lift my head and tap the tip of his nose.

"Och, is 'at whit yoo're tryin' tae dae?" Roban growls. He sits up and rolls me onto my back, my small, pointed breasts peering at the ceiling. He cups one peak and takes it into his warm, dewy mouth, his tongue drawing circles around my nipple.

I squirm and let out a moan before reluctantly pushing him away. My body begs for him once more, but it's morning and we both have work to do.

"If you keep that up, I'll never leave this bed again," I

say. I kiss him lightly on the cheek, a thank you for the wonderful night before.

"Is 'at a promise?" he says, slapping my bum.

I did have fun. A lot of it. Roban is a very generous lover to say the least, and waking up beside him makes my stomach flutter. Before our date, I found it hard to place how I felt about him. My guard was up, and rightfully so considering my past. But now, I feel ready to let all of that go. I am still damaged and I am still healing, but it seems like Roban is mending me at the broken places.

I'm not lying when I say I'll never leave my bed again so long as he is there beside me. But I can only ignore my financial woes for so long. I have big dreams for myself and my art, and I promised myself that I wouldn't get distracted from that. And if you can't keep promises with yourself, your word doesn't amount to anything at all.

With this in mind, I honor the vision I have for my future by sliding out of bed and gliding on my underwear and a loose-fitting painting dress. Roban looks at me with pleading eyes, but he knows he has to work, as well. I leave him to get dressed and go put on a pot of coffee.

There is a cup waiting for him on the counter when he finally emerges from the bedroom. He cups it into his hands, taking neither cream nor sugar, and kisses me on the cheek. There are so many words that we both want to say to one another, but instead, we keep those feelings inside, where they are felt but not flaunted. *Love is patient, love is kind. It does not envy, it does not boast, it is not proud,* I think to myself. I remember those words spoken from David's lips during his vows at our wedding. Yet, at every given opportunity, his love was demanding and self-serving. This is different. At least, I hope it is.

I sit in silence, scrolling through Facebook and Instagram as I drink my coffee. Roban does the same, though without peering over his shoulder, it's hard to say what he is doing on his phone. Occasionally he will whistle or clear his throat, but for the most part, he is silent, too. I like this. This ability to exist in our own worlds without depending on one another.

After about thirty minutes, we both finish our coffee and Roban heads toward the front door. I follow him until he turns around and faces me, placing his hands on my hips and pulling me to him. I look up into his glacial blue eyes as they stare directly into my soul. I feel seen and appreciated, which is new for me.

"You better get going, the crew is already here," I say, urging him to go but wishing he would stay.

"Aye, yoo're reit," he says, "But th' guid news is 'at we ooght tae finish yer yard today. Ah bit yoo're excited abit 'at."

I stand on my tip toes and kiss him on the lips. "Excited, but also sad. I won't get to watch you work anymore."

"Ye watch me wark?" he asks, teasing me.

"Of course I do. I paint with the curtains open. It's impossible not to look."

Roban chuckles. "Ye ken, Ah aye felt loch Ah was bein' watched. Noo Ah ken."

As much as I want Roban to stay, to climb back into bed with me, I also want him to leave so that I can spill my thoughts onto a canvas. I've never felt more inspired to paint. And with Margaret Conway's check coming in the mail, I can afford to take a day off from doing commissions and paint something for me—or rather, something for Roban.

He runs his hand through my hair and kisses my forehead. "I'll see ye later, lass."

"Not if I see you first," I joke, "Because, you know." I nod toward the dining room containing my easel and a paint-stained sheet draped over the hardwood floors.

Roban hesitates, but he opens the front door, calls out to his team, and shuts the door behind him, leaving me in solitude for at least the next few hours until Alice wakes up. I wonder if she knows that Roban spent the night. His motorcycle parked out front surely tipped her off. I won't hear the end of it once she's up. But what can I say? That she was right about Roban? I could never give her that satisfaction.

I enter the dining room and throw open the tangerine curtains. Already, I see that the landscapers are making good progress burying the new plants. It won't take them long. So, as I watch Roban kneeling in the rocks, his bare hands patting down the rich soil around each baby yucca and butterfly bush, I take out an array of paints: alizarin crimson, cadmium yellow, titanium white, and phthalo blue. As I mix colors on my palette with a knife, Vanta rubs against my bare legs and jumps into the windowsill. It seems as if she likes to watch the men work, as well. I'm in a chipper mood, so I return the affection by scratching her chin, accidentally leaving a smudge of light pink on her fur.

"It appears it's just you and me," I say aloud, sure that Vanta can understand me. I never thought I would be a pet person, but I have to admit, she's growing on me. Her constant company while I paint makes me feel less alone, which is something I didn't even know that I needed.

I cover the canvas with liquid clear before I start arranging the colors that I've mixed: varying shades of red, pink, purple, orange, and blue. I want to capture the essence of our perfect night at the aviary, with the setting sun and the carnal desire. I make large, sweeping brush strokes of pink and orange fading into purple and indigo to mimic the sunset, with amorphous shapes in an ardent shade of crimson, like the bright red patches on the foreheads of sandhill cranes.

It feels so good to paint expressive art. I haven't done it in years, so I admit I'm a little out of practice, but I love what I am creating. Mainly because I love the way it makes me feel when I look at it.

I'm startled when I hear the creaking floorboards behind me. When I turn around, I see Alice resting on the doorframe, smirking. I set down my palette and brush and put my hands on my hips.

"Go ahead. Say it," I say, "I know you want to."

Her smile grows wider. "Say what?"

I glare at her until she gives in.

"I take it you had a good night," she laughs.

I pick up my paints again and turn my back to her, shaking my head.

"Oh, Roban! Oh, Roban!" she moans in jest. I toss an unused paint brush in her direction, but I miss and it rolls across the floor. "Okay, okay. I'll leave you be. But not before telling you I told you so!"

Alice exits the room and goes into the kitchen. I can hear her rustling around in the cupboards, probably trying to scrounge up a late breakfast. I get back to work.

I am so involved in the act of creation that I don't even notice when the landscapers leave. Once I look out the window and see the white truck is gone, I leave my painting to dry, put on my house shoes, and walk out to the patio to observe their hard work.

I know it was more than just Roban, but I can't believe my yard's transformation over these last few weeks. What was once a dying lawn, scraggly bushes, and a sick tree is now a stylish spread of granite rock, spiky desert flora, and a brand new chokecherry sapling that I had watched Roban plant himself.

I descend the porch steps and walk out to the little sapling. Even though it is small right now, I feel lighter knowing that it will grow into a stronger, healthier tree than the one before it. So long as I remember to water it, nurture it, it will be better than ever. In time, I won't even remember the sick tree that once stood in my front yard. I won't remember how I clung to it for sentiment. I'll only remember the lovely Scottish gardener that I hissed at, and the new tree that he planted. There is only room for new growth.

As I stand in my yard, ignoring the fact that I am not wearing a bra and am covered in paint, Roban pulls up to the curb in his motorcycle. I smile as he removes his helmet and dismounts the bike. He's clearly gone home to shower and change clothes since his hair is wet and he is wearing a new plaid button-up and immaculate denim.

"Weel, whit dae ye hink?" he calls across the small yard.

I don't think. I don't answer. I just run across the cement path and jump into his arms. He catches me, holding my backside as my legs wrap around his waist. We swap kisses. It's hard to tell who missed whom more, him or me.

"I love it!" I finally say, pressing my mouth to his once more. I clamber down from Roban and lead him to the sapling. "You did this."

"Och, weel it wasn't jist me, lass," he says, nervously fidgeting with his man bun.

I click my tongue at him. "Nice try, Mr. Modest, but I saw you plant this tree yourself."

"It jist felt loch Ah shoods, efter cuttin' doon th' other one."

I weave my fingers through his, encouraging him to look down at me with my soft gaze. "I'm glad it was you."

His hand squeezes mine as I walk us to the porch. "Will you come inside? I want to show you something."

Roban nods and together we enter the newly restored bungalow. I get excited and pull him to the dining room. On the easel, likely near dry at this point, is my abstract painting inspired by our night together.

"I made this for you," I say. I'm smiling so big that my cheeks ache. I can't remember the last time that happened.

Roban stands still, eyeing the painting in either scrutiny or admiration. Which, I cannot tell. Then, without saying a word, he withdraws his cell phone from his pocket and snaps a picture of the painting.

"Why are you taking a picture? You can take this with you," I say, a little worried that I'm about to be rejected. Maybe it was too much, to paint him a painting. *Stupid, stupid, stupid.*

"It won't fit oan th' bike, lass," he says matter of factly. "But," he sidles up close to me, "Ah loove it. Nae sure Ah kin it, but Ah can appreciate it aw th' same."

He never explains the photo, and I don't have the heart to press the matter further. Instead, I offer him a glass of wine and insist that we sit out on the patio, like we used to, where it all started. Instead of sitting side by side on the Adirondack chairs, we both take a seat on the porch swing.

"Sae that's whit ye actually loch tae paint?" Roban asks after a moment of silence.

"Yeah," I say, "I suppose so."

"Abstract art?" he clarifies.

"Yes?"

"An' ye want yer wark displayed in a gallery? What's stoppin' ye frae daein' 'at?"

I ponder this a moment. "I guess nothing really is stopping me, besides these damn portrait commissions. And the fact that there are hardly any galleries in Salt Lake City. They're typically reserved for art students or visiting artists. It's hard for me to put myself out there when I'm so certain that I'll be met with rejection."

"Hae ye thooght abit submittin' yer wark tae galleries ootside ay Utah?"

I admit, the prospect of displaying and selling my work in a larger city thrills me. But then I think of my aging mother and I know that I can't leave Utah. I can't leave *her*.

"I don't think that's possible," I say.

"Wa nae, yoo're a talented painter, Ah don't see wa—"

"I can't leave Utah. Not after how hard I fought for this house. Not with my mother's questionable health. It's bad enough she lives hours away. If something happened to her, I could never forgive myself."

I feel my eyes starting to well up. I quickly blink away the tears and take a deep breath. Unfortunately, Roban notices and sets down his wine so he can clasp my hands, so small compared to his.

"I'm sae sorry, Emily," he whispers, "Ah didn't mean anythin' by it. Ah jist want tae dae everythin' Ah can tae help ye be whaur ye want tae be. If 'at means stayin' in Utah, I'm haur tae help ye figure 'at it."

I lean my head on his shoulder and just sit with my feelings of grief, worry, and anxiety. I allow myself to feel things for once, which is odd at first, but then a calm settles over me. I know I am not alone. For the first time, someone is on my team, rooting for me to achieve my dreams. But then again, is he really?

ten

ROBAN and I sit on the porch swing, swaying back and forth, until the sun dips below the horizon. A breeze has swept over the Salt Lake valley, and with it comes a blanket of smoke from the wildfires, trapped in the city by the towering mountain ranges in each direction. The sunset is blood red, not like the kaleidoscopic colors of the sunset at the aviary the night before.

Though I am calm, there is still an annoying pin prick in my brain urging me to fight or fly. I try to swallow those feelings with varying degrees of success, depending on how long we sit in silence and I am left to dwell on my thoughts. Occasionally, Roban will recite a line from a poem or tell me that it will be okay and things will work out the way I want them to, and that distracts me for a time. But then our words cease and my thoughts flow like torrential downpour, like a flash flood in the red-rock desert.

Still, Roban is helping me get out of my head a little bit and talk about my concerns. He tries to offer solutions, but I secretly dismiss them. He means well, I know he does, but all I really need is for someone to sit with the discomfort and tell me that everything sucks. Maybe I'm being a martyr. I don't care. I just need to acknowledge what's eating at me and keep living out of spite.

"Ur ye hungry?" Roban asks. "Mebbe we coods grab a late dinner?"

I think about this for a minute, mentally scanning my body to determine what it wants. But all I really want is for my mother to be well and for my paintings to sell.

"No thanks. I'm not hungry."

"Weel, is thaur anythin' Ah can dae tae help?" he says.

This ignites a fury within me. I don't know why. In my heart, I know he is trying to be kind and considerate, but it's also bothersome to hear I am something that needs to be fixed.

I remove my hand from his, unweaving our fingers and snatching my body back from his gentle grip. "No," I snap, "I don't need your help."

"I'm sorry, Emily. Ah jist—"

"You just what? You want to jump into my life and be the solution to all of my problems? I don't need saving."

My eyes are burning as they stare at Roban, who is looking down at his feet and biting at his lower lip. He is clearly hurt and I almost feel bad for yelling at him. I've never seen him like this. Even when I shouted at him about cutting down my tree over the sound of buzzing chainsaws, he didn't look so defeated. He rose to meet my anger and shouted right back at me. I see there is no fight left in this man.

"I'm sorry," I whisper, reaching back for his hand.

The corner of his mouth curls into a stoic smile and he wraps his fingers around mine.

"It's okay, lass. I'm sorry fur upsettin' ye."

We swing together in silence for a long time. All I can

think about is whether I was justified in my anger. That, and wondering what Roban is thinking. I know he is a sweet man, but God, it is so much to take in. I wouldn't go so far as to say that I thrive on neglect, but I need my space. I need my independence. Without this, I'm afraid I will fall in love again and lose myself in the process. I can't have that. It happened once with David and I'll be damned if it happens again.

I don't know what Roban wants, and that's what scares me most of all. I assume, like David, that he wants to possess me, to control me, domesticate me. But I refuse to be tamed. For the first time in more than a decade, I am free to be my own person. I am free to have goals and work to achieve them without my ambitions being ridiculed. What does anyone want from another person? Aren't we all out here competing for personal gain? What does Roban expect of me?

"It's getting late," I say, interrupting the stillness.

"Aye," says Roban, "Yoo're reit. Maybe we shoods go inside an' gie some sleep?"

I let out a deep sigh. "Roban, I think I should just be alone tonight."

He looks shocked. Puzzled, even. "Sorry, Ah didn't mean tae assume—"

"Maybe you shouldn't have assumed," I say, surprising even myself with my cold demeanor. "I told you I had conditions if we were going to see each other. Part of that included giving me my space."

Roban pulls his hair back and secures it into a bun, his brow furrowed and the corners of his mouth turned down.

"If ye need yer space, Ah guess that's fine," he says.

"You guess?"

"Look, Ah didn't mean anythin' by 'at. It's just—I want

tae see ye, Emily. Ah want tae spend time wi' ye."

"Maybe later," I say, feeling my fuse fizzle out, "I just really need some alone time tonight. We'll see each other again soon, I promise."

Roban kisses me lightly on the cheek and steps down off the porch. He begins walking to his motorcycle, but then he turns around and says, "Ah rilly hope ye loch th' yard."

My throat feels tight and it hurts to swallow, like there is a lump in my throat. "Good night, Roban."

"Guid night, lass."

Roban swings his leg over his motorcycle, revs the engine, and pulls away from the curb, leaving behind the sound of thunder that gets weaker and weaker the farther his silhouette disappears under the streetlights.

I feel awful, but I need some time to keep my wits about me. I could sense myself catching feelings for him, and there is no truer sign of clear and present danger. That's how it all starts. Then I blink and a decade of my life is gone with nothing to show for it. I need to tread lightly, only dipping my toes in the shallow water and not diving right into the deep end.

I walk back inside and lock the door behind me. Alice is sitting with her feet up on the couch reading a book. I stare at her until she looks up from her book and tilts her head. It's not until she has hurriedly set the book down and rushed over to my side that I realize that I am crying.

Alice hugs me tight before leaning away to get a better look at me. Her eyes examine my damp face like those of a doctor, trying to catch a glimpse of what ails me.

"Honey, what is wrong?" she says.

"I—I don't know," I sob. "One moment, everything was fine, and then Roban and I talked about my mother and—"

"Shh... shh..." Alice coos, petting my head as she pulls

me back into a hug. "It's okay. Just take a couple of deep breaths. We're going to get through this."

I heed her words and inhale, exhale, inhale, exhale.

"Good. Now start from the beginning."

Words come spilling out like water from a broken fire hydrant. Words that have been pent up for months. I begin by talking about my painting aspirations again (after all, Alice has heard this a million times before) and then my vision for the future. Then I tell her all the barriers keeping me from making that vision a reality, including my mother, including Roban.

I try to explain it all, and Alice simply nods and listens. When I am done and the tears have stopped dripping off my chin, Alice takes a deep breath and slaps me right across the face.

"Ouch! What was that for?" I shout. I reach for her with both of my hands, but she catches them by the wrists and wrestles them back until I give up and stuff my hands into my dress pockets.

"You're being a whiny twat," she says matter-of-factly. "You are creating problems for yourself that don't even exist yet. Stop living in the past and the future and meet me here, in the present."

I look down. My cheek is hot and it stings from her slap. I am equal parts angry and ashamed.

"Listen, babe. You've got two options: break things off with Roban and devote your life to being a spinster—even after your mom is gone—and struggle with your art. Or—I can't believe I'm saying this—you can fall in love for real this time, with someone that respects you and wants to see you thrive, to help you with your mother, and to help you with your art," she says.

"Are those my only two options?" I sniff.

"You've got to learn how to ask for help," she says, "There's no shame in that."

She's right. I hate that she's right. I've been so focused on being self-reliant that I haven't been willing to ask for help from the people that matter. Being an only child, I have to find someone to help with my mother. And being a poor artist, I need someone to help my career flourish. Clearly Alice thinks Roban is the one to help with both of these things, but I'm a bit more skeptical. *David, maybe...* No. Not David. I know he knows my family and at least seemed to care about them, but I couldn't ask him for anything. Not after the divorce.

"Alice," I say, "Couldn't you just help me?"

She laughs and clasps my hands. "Babe, you know I will be here for you until hell freezes over. You can always count on me to help. I just can't promise that it will be enough."

I twist my brow. "What do you mean?"

Alice steeples her hands and presses them to her lips in thought. Finally, she lets out a sigh. "Emily, there are things you will need that I can't give you. I love you to death, but also, I have my own life and I need to live it. Roban can—"

I stop her right there. "If things with Roban are going to work, he and I both need to have our own lives. So why can't I just be the spinster with the devoted friend instead?"

"Either way, you're depending on someone, right? I thought that wasn't what you wanted."

Damn it. She's right again. How must it feel to be so right all of the time? Call me stubborn, but I decide to push back on it.

"Isn't asking for help just depending on another person to solve your problems?" I ask.

"No," says Alice, "It's simply accepting your own limitations. You can be alone, sure. But you need a partner of some kind to help get you over this hurdle. I've got my own shit going on, Emily. And quite frankly, you need to give as much as you take. I will always be there for you, but if you're going to depend on me, I need to be able to depend on you. Does that make sense?"

"It does," I confess. "I guess I've been a really shitty friend."

Alice clicks her tongue. "No, no, no. Not shitty. Just... self-contained."

It's just a nice way of her telling me I've been selfish, but it's always been tough love with Alice. She calls me out on my bullshit and I try to become a better person. That's why I need her, and I'm a little upset that she's unwilling to become a spinster too and be my platonic partner. It would make things so much easier if romance wasn't part of the equation. I know it's intimacy that scares me, but I'm sure Alice would say that I need to work through that somehow. She wants to pawn me off onto Roban. Can't say I blame her. I really have been a shitty friend.

"I'm sorry I wasn't there for you during your breakup with Zach," I say, my eyes glossy with regret. "I was going through the divorce and I know that isn't a good excuse, it's just hard for me to see when I am needed."

Alice places her hand on my shoulder. "It's okay. I got through it. Plus, you gave me somewhere to live. If that isn't looking out for a friend, I don't know what is."

I laugh, "You're the one doing me a favor. I can't afford this house alone."

"Maybe one day we'll be homeless together. You, a starving artist. Me, an undervalued teacher," she says, cracking a smile. "But in the meantime, you really should give Roban a chance to help you."

"I guess," I sigh. "But if you see any red flags, you have

to tell me. You know I can't see those things by myself."

"Deal." Alice shakes my hand with a firm and vigorous grip. "Now I better be off to bed. Don't make any rash decisions while I am asleep."

Alice throws me a wink and disappears into her bedroom, closing the door behind her.

I pour myself another glass of wine and throw it back like I'm pounding a shot of liquor. This is a lot to take in. I don't mean to be selfish. Admitting that I've been emotionally unavailable to my best friend is hard. It makes me wonder what else I have missed, who else I have hurt. I hope that I've been a better daughter than a friend. Even with my mother more than two-hundred miles away, I do try to see her often. Even when I was with David, I saw her at least once a year, which I realize now is abysmal, but I really did try. Had I known that her health would deteriorate so quickly, I would have visited more. I mean, the tremors? What is happening with her? Hindsight is twenty-twenty. The best I can do now is be present for her now before it's too late.

As for Roban, I will keep trying, but I need my personal space and freedom. I can't be tied down every night just to binge watch the latest series on Netflix every night of the week. But also, I do crave companionship and I know that I need it in a way that Alice cannot provide. So, I will keep seeing Roban so long as he respects my boundaries. Likewise, I will try to be conscious of his needs, but not if it means sacrificing my own instead.

I empty my wine glass down the sink and put it in the dishwasher. I've had enough for tonight. For now, I need rest. So, I climb into bed and stare at the ceiling, frantically replaying every mistake I've ever made in my head. I close my eyes and pray for sleep.

eleven

I SPEND the morning painting something new. It's dark and perhaps a bit violent with its splashes of midnight black and crimson. It takes me all afternoon to finish it and by the time I am finished, I feel a little better—but I want to paint over the canvas and start over. I can't seem to transpose my emotions onto the blank slate in front of me. I've never had this problem before. I'm usually pretty self-aware; I meditate frequently, go on walks, and say what's on my mind. Things are best dealt with outside in the open, but for some reason, I seem to be holding something back.

Still, Alice slapped some sense into me last night. I am determined to be a better person, and to do that, I need to be present for my loved ones. I have lived in the shadow of my divorce for too long. It's time to rise above it and move on with my life.

To begin, I decide to make a few overdue phone calls. The first number I dial is my mother's.

The phone rings for so long, I'm surprised it doesn't go to voicemail. But at long last, she picks up, much to my own relief.

"Emily? Is everything okay?" she asks.

I'm not entirely sure how to answer that. Besides, I haven't called to talk about myself. I want to talk about her. "Everything is fine, Mom. I just wanted to call and check up on you."

I hear her full-bellied laughter on the other line.

"Mom, what is so funny?"

"Oh, Robert just made a funny joke," she says.

Robert. Of course she's with Robert. I hate to admit it, but it's probably for the best. I don't want her to be alone in her condition. Still, I wish Robert would disappear. We've got things under control.

"Robert's with you?" I ask, trying to mask my disappointment.

"Of course he is, honey. Now, what do you need?"

I hate that she assumes I need something, but it only confirms what Alice told me last night. I need to give as much as I take, so I'm going to start making the effort.

"I just wanted to chat, but if this isn't a good time—"

"I can talk for a little bit, I suppose," she says.

Although she has agreed to speak with me, it feels like I am imposing when Robert is hovering somewhere nearby.

"So," I say, "How are you doing?"

I want to broach the subject of Parkinson's, but I don't know how to do it delicately. I'm afraid that reminding her of her disease will just upset her.

"I'm fine, Emily. Really. I told you, you don't need to worry about me. The doctor prescribed some medications to help with the tremors. Besides that, there's nothing we can really do except wait," she says.

Wait for what? I want to ask. For the disease to take over? For her to lose her independence? For death? I don't want to think about it, but I know it's something that both my mother and I need to deal with.

"Is there anything I can do for you? Anything at all?"

"No, Emily," she sighs, "I'm doing as well as can be expected. The best thing you can do for me right now is to go on living your life. Keep creating and open your heart to others. That's all I ask."

"Okay," I say, "I'll let you go."

"I'll tell Robert you say hi."

"Please do," I say, gritting my teeth. But she's already hung up the phone.

I need to mentally compose myself before I make my next phone call. I don't know why I always forget how much talking to my mother takes out of me. It didn't always used to be this way. Something about our relationship changed when I got married. Or maybe it was just before that, when my father died. We used to rely on one another. But then our dynamic shifted. Perhaps I needed more than she was able to give. Perhaps I didn't give as much as she needed. Somewhere along the line, we stopped depending on each other, even when things got tough. I'd say I mourn the days when we were best friends that would turn to each other for every little thing, but here we are: alive, breathing, and mostly unscathed. The last decade has taught us resilience. I should have more faith in her ability to take care of herself, at least for now.

The next phone call I make is to Roban. I could tell he was hurt last night and that it was my fault. It's just that I don't know how to mask my emotions. Words come tumbling out, and even though I usually mean them, I could do so with a bit more tact. Then there's my anger. I don't know who I am angry at, but Roban doesn't deserve to be at the receiving end of it. So, I press the call button and wait. It wouldn't surprise me if he didn't answer. I wouldn't blame him.

But almost immediately, he picks up.

"Hello," he says in a low, gravelly voice.

"Hi, Roban," I say genially. Silence on the other end. I decide to cut to the chase. "Listen, I am sorry for how I acted last night. I'm stressed about money and angry about my mother's condition, and none of that should have been directed at you. Can we get some coffee and talk?"

"Sure," he says simply. I can tell he is still hurt. I have to make amends.

"Meet me at Sugar House Coffee?" I plead.

"Okay. I'll see ye thaur in a bit."

He hangs up. The tension over the phone line was thick as molasses. I am desperate to fix things. I'm not ready to let Roban go.

WHEN I ARRIVE at the coffee shop, I don't see Roban. Makes sense. I live down the street, he lives on the other side of the valley. I order an iced chai latte and take a seat at a table nearest to the door. I almost finish my beverage before I see him approaching on the other side of the glass door. He swings it open and I wave timidly at him. He doesn't smile.

"Whit ur ye drinkin'?" he asks. "Can Ah gie ye anither?"

"Iced chai latte," I say, slurping the last drops from the bottom of the cup. "Thank you."

He stands in line and I awkwardly thread my fingers together over and over. My palms are sweaty and it is uncomfortably hot with the summer sun blasting through the window beside me. *What if he doesn't forgive me?* I wonder. The thought makes me perspire even more.

"Haur ye go," he says, setting a full cup in front of me. He sits across from me and sets his phone and a large, steaming cup of tea on the table. "Sae?"

"So," I begin. I want to be deliberate with my words. I can't risk hurting him again. "I want to apologize for my behavior last night. I snapped at you and misdirected my anger towards you and for that I am very, very sorry."

Roban takes a quick sip of his tea and ponders this for a moment. "It's nae jist yer words 'at hurt me, Emily. It's hoo ye act aroond me. One moment, it seems loch ye want tae be wi' me, an' th' next, Ah am discarded loch auld produce. Ah can't jist be an occasional need fur ye. Ah ken ye need ur space, an' Ah respect 'at, but Ah need reassurance coz if yoo're nae aroond—" he sighs, "When yoo're nae aroond, I'm afraid yoo've moved oan entirely."

Roban stares at a knot in the wooden table top, his calloused fingers anxiously rubbing the groove. I reach across the space between us and take his hand.

"What do you need from me, Roban? I'll try to be more conscious of your needs, but first, I have to know what those are," I say softly. I gently caress his knuckle before giving his hand a tight squeeze.

Roban looks up from the table and gazes straight into my eyes. "Ah want tae be wi' ye, Emily. Ah want ye tae want tae be wi' me. Ah want tae spend mair time wi' ye withit bein' tauld tae leave when ye tire ay me. Ah want ye tae be th' lest thin' Ah see when Ah go tae sleep an' th' first thin' Ah see when Ah wauk'. An' Ah want ye tae be present when I'm thaur. I'm sure it seems loch I'm askin' fur a lot, but—"

"Roban," I say, "I do want to be with you. I'll try harder. I promise."

He cracks a smile and clasps my outstretched hand in both of his, dwarfing my fingers with their tremendous size. It makes me feel small and safe, like all of my problems can't find me when I am protected by his gentle touch.

"Thenk ye," he says. "Ah ken Ah can be *a lot*, but ever since Sophie broke aff uir engagement, I've bin afraid tae pit myself it thaur coz Ah hink 'at jist when things ur gettin' guid, I'm gonnae be abandoned yit again. Ah don't ken if Ah can handle 'at."

"So long as you are respectful and communicate with me, I don't see myself abandoning you," I swear. "I'm damaged, too, remember? But I can't let that get in the way of my own happiness. We have to learn to trust again."

"Whit is loove withit troost?" Roban grins.

I nod. There it is. *Love.* The thing I fear most, and now the word is just hanging in the air like some kind of phantom. Does Roban *love* me? So soon? I have feelings for Roban, but I don't know if it's as strong as love. Not yet.

"Yer hands ur ice cold," Roban says. He rubs his palm against my skin to gather warmth.

"Must just be the air conditioning in here," I lie. But I know the truth. That word is haunting me, and I'll admit, I am absolutely terrified.

I take a long sip of my chai latte and quickly try to change the subject.

"So what does Roban do on a lazy Saturday?" I ask.

"I'd hardly caa it lazy. Ah spent most ay th' day wood-workin' in th' garage," he says.

"Woodworking? Like what?"

"Aw sorts ay things: dressers, tables, chairs. Furniture, mainly."

"Here I thought you just liked botany and poetry. You're

full of surprises," I laugh. "How did you get into woodworking?"

"Mah grandad showed me hoo when Ah was wee. Probably tay wee tae be workin' wi' power tools, but he helped me build whatever Ah dreamed ay. Ah jist loch creatin' things, whether it's a manicured garden ur a humble bookcase. That's part ay whit drew me tae ye. Ye loch creatin', tay."

"We're a dying breed," I joke. "People these days like buying mass produced art on Etsy and bargain furniture from Ikea."

Roban nods in agreement.

I want to talk to him more about his woodworking, but I am interrupted by a vibration on the table as I take a breath to speak. My eyes dart towards Roban's cell phone. The screen reads "Incoming Call: Ainsley".

"Ah shoods tak' thes," Roban says as he rises from his seat. He picks up his phone and goes outside to answer.

Who is Ainsley? It dawns on me that this isn't the first time Roban's had to duck out for a call. Is it always Ainsley? Is she a friend? A girlfriend? Hell, a wife? I rule out the last possibility since I've seen his house. It's clear that only men live there.

I watch Roban as he talks to Ainsley. He's more animated than usual, gesticulating wildly with his empty hand and a huge smile spread across his face. I've never seen him so happy. Not since that call at the aviary. A pang of jealousy rolls through my body like thunder. I can hear David's clinical voice in my head: *Don't catastrophize everything. Decide whether what you are feeling is rational.* I shake this all from my mind.

I'm sure I have nothing to worry about with Roban. He said himself that he wants to be with me. I need to trust him and take him at his word. Still... There are some lingering doubts.

Roban comes back inside and takes a seat. He takes a large draft of his tea.

I see that he isn't going to address who called him, so I dismiss it from my brain. I decide that I want him. All of him. Right now. He's looking at me with those big, arctic eyes and I am consumed with this longing to connect, to touch, to possess. I want to remind him that I am here for him and only him. It's scary to think about, and I can already feel myself leaving my body. Lust has taken over, and everything else that matters to me—my mom, my art, my house—simply disappears.

"Sorry abit 'at," he says. "Whaur waur we?"

"Creation," I say. But in my mind, we are already in bed, his warm body pressed against mine, our legs tangled in the sheets.

"Och, aye. Yoo're reit. Th' hin' Ah loch abit creatin' is—"

"Do you want to get out of here?" I ask.

He looks surprised, but it quickly melts into a suggestive smirk. He doesn't need to answer for me to know he is completely on board. He gulps the remaining bit of tea in his cup and takes my hand. He leads me to the door, which he courteously opens for me, and down the sidewalk in the direction of the bungalow.

There's no shade as we walk down the street. Nowhere to hide from the searing summer heat. Our palms sweat as they meld together. Despite the slickness of our hands, we will not let go. We're laughing as we walk, steps in sync with one another, drawing nearer and nearer to the bungalow. We both know what is about to happen, and the very thought of it makes us blush, or perhaps that is just a burn from the sun.

"Ah cannae bide tae tear 'at frock aff ay ye," Roban growls, leaning close into my loose hair.

"And I cannot wait to rip the buttons off of your shirt," I laugh. I give his button-up a little tug.

Soon, thanks to our eager gait, the bungalow is within eyesight. Roban scoops me up in his arms and begins carrying me to the house. I giggle and squirm, pounding lightly on his broad chest.

"Put me down! I can manage twenty steps," I say in jest.

"If ye didne want tae be picked up, ye shooldnae be sae bonnie an' wee," he says. He grasps my thighs a little bit tighter, squeezes my body a little bit closer, as he ascends the front porch steps and sets me down in front of the door.

My hands are trembling with excitement as I sort through my keys to try to find the right one. It takes a minute, but I finally grip it and slide it into the lock, turning frantically and shoving my body weight into the door to make it budge. The door swells during the summer, making it difficult to push open, but with both Roban and myself forcing it, it swings open and I lead Roban by his shirt collar inside. He's removing my dress before we even get a chance to shut and lock the door.

twelve

IT'S LATE when I awake. I reach across the chasm of the bed, hoping to run my fingers through Roban's chest hair, but instead all I feel are cool empty sheets. I sit up, rubbing the sleep from my eyes, looking for any sign of Roban. He isn't here.

I slip my yellow mandala dress over my head and smooth the thin fabric down with my hands to eliminate any static before walking into the kitchen to look for Roban. Still, he is nowhere to be seen. There is, however, a note by the coffee maker.

Emily, it reads, *I didn't want to wake you. I thought you might need some space so you can paint or do anything else that your heart desires. Thinking of you, Roban.*

My heart stops pounding and a calm settles over me. I'm impressed. I thought my conversation with him yesterday would mean making sacrifices, but at least right now, he is respecting my boundaries. *This is good,* I think. And it is. Alice was right, as usual, about me needing to step up and give as much as I take. It seems Roban and I have found a compromise that works for both of us.

I put on a pot of coffee for Alice and I to drink, and just in time, because she drowsily creeps into the kitchen and sits at the island counter clutching her head in her hands.

"Late night?" I ask, handing her a mug of black coffee.

She simply grunts and takes a sip.

"Was it your book or something else?" I inquire further.

"Something else," she says. "You and Roban sure know how to deprive a woman of sleep."

I chuckle and twist a strand of my light brown hair in front of my face. "I thought you would be happy for me," I say.

Alice blows into her mug to try to cool the coffee. "I'm happy for you, but my God, Emily, you two go at it for hours. At least learn how to keep it down."

I sense that her frustrations go deeper than just sleep deprivation. "What else is bothering you? You seem... unwell."

Alice takes a sip and her face turns pale green. "I think I'm going to throw up," she says.

I stand away from the sink as she rises from her seat and runs over to empty her stomach into the basin. When she's done, she stands up straight and turns on the faucet, sending all remains of her vomit down the drain. She clutches her stomach and sits back down, cradling her head in both hands.

"I drank too much last night," she admits.

"Oh?" I ask, "What was the occasion?"

"I had a date," she says, "Met a girl at the pub down the street."

This is surprising to me considering how heartbroken she was when she moved in months ago. Her ex-boyfriend, Zach, was fine. I wasn't crazy about him, but he made Alice happy, and so that was enough for me. He never did anything to hurt Alice when they were together, but then he got a job opportunity out of state and that was that. He left her behind and she swore off love at the same time I did. I suppose seeing me with Roban must make her feel especially lonely. I didn't think about that.

"A girl this time, huh?" I say.

"Yeah," says Alice, "Women are much more reliable. Men are fickle."

"Cheers! Here's hoping we get things right this time around." I lift up my mug and Alice does the same. "I take it the date went well if you drank that much."

Alice dry heaves at the very mention of drinking. "Please. I don't want to think about it."

"Alright, I won't, but talk to me. I want to know everything!" I say, leaning forward onto the counter.

Alice collects herself by running her hands through her hair and lightly slapping her cheeks. "Her name is Jessica. She's an attorney for an environmental nonprofit. Her job is boring as hell, but she sure knows how to knock back a shot of tequila. Make that a dozen shots of tequila." Alice retches again.

"How did you meet?" I ask. "Tinder?"

"No, it's through this app called HER. It's geared toward queer women like me. You probably wouldn't have heard of it."

"Yeah, you're right," I laugh, shaking off my ignorance.

"Anyway, we stayed at the pub until closing time, which should tell you a lot considering you and I both know that I go to bed at nine o'clock unless I can't stop working on my book. Jessica was a lot of fun, but I'm not sure if that's what I'm looking for right now," Alice sighs.

"What *are* you looking for?"

She sets her cup down and looks directly at me, tilting her head. "You really don't know?"

I am perplexed. I shake my head and peer at her warily.

"I want what you and I have, but... more," she says, averting her gaze. "You and I have been friends forever, and I think that's great, but there have been times when I've wished we were more than friends. I'm sorry if that makes you uncomfortable, I just—"

"Alice," I say. "It's okay. I already know."

"You do?"

"Yes," I reach over and set my hand on her shoulder, chuckling to myself. "It's fine, really. If I liked girls, believe me, you'd be at the top of my list."

Alice's cheeks turn bright pink. "You mean that?"

"Yes, definitely."

I AM CHIPPER THIS MORNING, and I suppose I have Roban to thank for that. I decide to start a new abstract painting just for me. I mix Indian yellow with bright red oil paint, sap green with prussian blue. The way I see it, there are two versions of me: the person that I used to be when I was married to David, and the person I am now, happy and free. I want to paint this dichotomy with colors that will complement my house, which is strangely lacking in art despite my living here. I choose a bright orange, like the curtains in the dining room, and a deep turquoise like the new sheets on my bed. Half of the canvas is orange, the other half teal, with overlapping squares where they meet in the middle, making it hard to tell where one color ends and another begins. I am just putting on the finishing touches when I feel my phone vibrate in my dress pocket.

I hear a knock on the door and instead of checking my video doorbell app like I usually do, I rush to the door, unlocking it quickly so I can let who could only be Roban inside to see what I made. But no. As I swing the door open, I am met by the clean-cut face of my ex-husband.

"Hi," he says, waving his hand awkwardly. He's wearing a blue button-up shirt with a black striped tie and perfectly tailored gray slacks. He always looks so put together. It's one of the things that makes him so intimidating.

I think about slamming the door in his face. In fact, I begin to close the door, but his hand catches it and pushes it back open and before I know it, David is standing inches in front of me.

"David," I say, "This isn't a good time."

"Is it ever a good time?" he says. "You've been screening my calls for months. Can I please just come in?"

As if I can say no with his hand on the door. I gesture towards the couch so he can take a seat. He kicks off his shoes and enters and suddenly I feel like I've been transported back to a time when we were still married and I was unhappy, though I couldn't pinpoint precisely why. I shut the door and stand before him.

"Please, Emily, can you sit so we can talk?" he says. Without thinking, I do as I'm told and sit on the couch beside him.

"What is this about, David?"

"I just wanted to see how you are doing," he says. This, I believe. Of course he would come to check in on me. Of course this isn't really over.

"I'm doing fine," I say. I try to look away, but his hand catches my cheek and he directs my face toward his.

"I don't believe you," he says. "You're holding something back. Tell me, what's the matter?"

I want to scream at him, to tell him that the only thing that is wrong is that my ex-husband is showing up at my house unannounced, but he and I both know that as much as I think these things, I can't say them aloud. Not in front of him. I never have.

Instead, a swell of emotions overtakes me and suddenly I am weeping in David's arms.

"It's okay," he says, rubbing my back, "It's okay. I'm here now."

Through the tears, everything comes rushing out.

"My mother has Parkinson's," I say. "She won't let me help. There's nothing I can do."

"How can *I* help?" David asks. I ponder this for a moment. Can he help? Should he help?

"Unless you can magically reverse her condition, I don't see how you can," I say. I wipe the tears from my face and wipe them on my dress.

"I know some neurologists," David says, "I could make some calls, get her better treatment here in the city."

His offer is tempting. Bringing my mother from Moab to Salt Lake City would make things a lot less stressful. Her treatment would be better, for starters, and I would be able to check in on her without making the three hour trek.

"You'd really do that?" I ask.

"Yes."

"Why?" Even though I can't voice my frustrations with David, I am still wary of his intentions.

"Because I want to help you, Emily." He reaches for my hand. "I've missed you."

Instead of recoiling, I sit there, frozen, and let him clasp my hand.

"Why did you do it?" I ask.

"Do what?" He blinks at me.

"Everything."

I'm sobbing again and David is holding my hand. I can feel myself in his grasp, unable to escape.

"I don't expect you to forgive me for what I did to you," he says. "Infidelity is untenable, I know that, but our marriage was falling apart and I made a mistake. You wouldn't even touch me, wouldn't look at me, and then I..." He trails off. "I want you back, Emily. I still think about you every day. I've been miserable without you. Please. I'm begging you to give me another chance."

He's staring at me expectantly with his piercing gaze. I want to tell him no, to fuck off, but I can't bring myself to say the words. They come up like bile and I choke. Instead, I don't say anything at all. I just sit there, unable to break eye contact with David, until he leans in and kisses me, gently at first and then forcefully, his tongue breaking through my closed lips. I do not kiss him back.

He leans away, still clutching my head with his hands.

"I don't expect you to give me an answer now. Just promise me you'll think about it," he says.

At last, he lets go and rises from the couch. Vanta enters the room, but her tail prickles and she walks with her back arched, hugging the walls as she steps along the perimeter of the room. David doesn't even notice her presence as he walks toward the door. He forces the swollen door open and stands in the passageway.

"I'll text you, okay?" he says.

I nod. But as he stands there looking at me, Vanta sneaks behind him and then bolts outside.

"Vanta!" I yelp and run towards the door. David looks confused. "David," I shout, "You let the cat out!"

"You have a cat?"

I shove him aside and stand on the porch with my bare

feet, looking for any sign of Vanta, but she is nowhere in sight.

"Shit," I mumble to myself.

"Sorry, I didn't mean to. I didn't know," David says. He looks down at his perfect leather loafers in dismay.

"I need you to leave," I say firmly. "I need to find my cat."

"I'm sure he'll be fine. Cats get outside all of the time." He sets his hand on my shoulder, which is more annoying than it is comforting.

"It's a she, and she's never been outside before. My God, David, she's just a kitten!" I'm seething and David's presence is not making me feel any better. "You can either help look for her or get out of my way."

David blinks wide at this. He is clearly stunned that I am bossing him around like this. In truth, it is very uncharacteristic of me when he is around, but I'm realizing just how important Vanta is to me. Even though I have only had her a few short weeks, she has grown on me. I love painting with her sitting on the windowsill, watching the birds and squirrels outside her reach. I guess she spent too much time yearning for outside, because given the chance, she quickly made her escape. Maybe I was wrong to take her in. Maybe she was meant to be feral all along. How does one temper a wild thing? Is it even possible?

I run inside and grab my keys and a pair of slip-on shoes that I keep near the entrance. As I'm collecting my things, I shout Alice's name until she sprints into the living room as if the house were on fire.

"What is it?" she asks frantically.

"Vanta is gone," I say, "Put on some shoes and let's go."

Alice runs to her room and returns in a flash. We step outside and I slam the door, locking it behind me. To

Emily's surprise, David is standing there on the porch, dumbfounded.

"David's here?" she asks, giving me a look of disapproval.

"Not now, Alice," I say, "Come on."

"I'll go this way, you two go the other?" David suggests.

I nod and side-step away from him with Alice in tow, running down the porch steps and onto the sidewalk, looking for any sign of my little black cat. I turn to see David walk the opposite direction. He's making *pspsps* sounds to try to lure Vanta to him, wherever she might be. But I know he'll never find her. If she decides to come at all, she'll only come for me or Alice. I pray we'll find her—more for my sake than her own.

thirteen

"SO, explain to me what David was doing at the house," Alice demands. We're walking slowly down the sidewalk calling for Vanta, but we both know it's no use. She's only little. She doesn't know her name, and it's not necessarily in a cat's nature to come when called. Still, maybe we will hear her mewing, maybe we will see her small fluffy body tucked away somewhere safe.

"I don't know. He just sort of... showed up," I say.

"And you let him *in*?"

I think about this a moment. How *did* he end up in the house? I don't remember inviting him in, but did he really force his way in? My thoughts are swimming. It's all very fuzzy.

"I—I don't think I did," I say, a little perplexed.

"That bastard," Alice scoffs, "He's so entitled that he thinks he can just barge into his ex-wife's house. I wonder what he wants."

I want to keep my mouth shut about what he told me. I feel like part of what transpired is my fault, like maybe I sent him mixed signals. But I can't keep anything from

Alice. Ever since we met in college, we have told each other everything.

"He said he wants me to give him another chance," I blurt out, almost by accident, but I know what I'm doing. I'm trying to get Alice involved so that she can sort out what happened because I certainly can't. Not by myself.

"He said *what*?" Alice stops walking and looks at me in disbelief. I shrug casually, but her forehead creases and she sneers. "And what did you say?"

"I didn't say anything," I protest, "At least, I don't think I did."

"Oh, I believe it," Alice says. "That's just like him. I swear, when you two are together, your mind goes blank because he's replacing your memories with his lies. You lose all ability to trust yourself. It's like brainwashing. He didn't try anything, did he?"

I look down at my slip-on shoes and kick at the ground. My face must betray me because I feel hot and flustered, but maybe that's just the summer heat getting to me.

"Oh my god, he did!" Alice shouts. She starts pacing back toward the house. "I swear, I'm going to kill him."

I grab her by the arm and stop her in her tracks.

"Alice, stop," I say. But Alice breaks away from my grip.

"Tell me what you remember," she commands.

"Give me a minute. I—I don't know," I cup my face in my hands and pull my hair out of my sweating face. I take stock of the situation. "Okay, he knocked on the door, I answered. He wanted to talk and I... I think I invited him inside. We sat on the couch. He asked about my mother and offered to help. He was being real nice, actually. But then, I don't know, the subject changed and he said he's sorry for cheating on me and begged for another chance. And then..."

I freeze.

"Then what?" Alice asks gently.

"He kissed me." I wince like Alice might slap me again, but as I close my eyes and wait for the sting of her palm, I hear her stomping away, back to the house. "Alice," I shout, chasing after her. "What are you going to do?"

"The nerve of that guy," she seethes. "He tries to control you for more than a decade, cheats on you, and then finally when you are happy, he decides to roll up and destroy everything. You do see that, right? You see what he's doing. He's trying to gain control again."

"I didn't kiss him back, Alice," I say, "He genuinely seemed heartbroken and he offered to make some calls around the hospital for my mom. I really think he's changed. Why can't we be friends?"

"Because, Emily," Alice stops and faces me. "You don't befriend your abuser."

There's that word again: *abuse*. It's such a heavy word, and I don't like to think of myself as a victim. Yes, David and I had a tumultuous relationship. But was what he did abuse? Alice seems to think so.

"Alice," I say, "Is this because you... like me?"

Her face turns white and her mouth drops open. "Are you fucking serious right now?"

"What? Doesn't it make sense that you would hate David because you have a crush on me?" I ask defensively.

"I hate David because he's an asshole, Emily. I wish that you could see that," she says. The corners of her eyes droop a little. She looks impossibly sad. "He got to your head by playing Mr. Nice Guy and now I can't believe you're defending him. I'll forgive you for what you said because you're clearly going through some shit right now, but don't for a second think I'm the one whose judgement is clouded. What about Roban? What are you going to tell him?"

Fuck. I completely forgot about Roban.

"I'll tell him the truth," I say.

"Will you?" Alice sighs. "Do you even know the truth?"

"Yes, I promise," I say. I don't want her to be mad at me. I need her right now more than anything else.

"Then call him right now and tell him," she says. She puts her hands on her hips and taps her foot on the pavement. I take my phone out of my pocket and stare at the black screen. "Well, are you going to do it or not?"

I unlock the phone and dial Roban's number. Alice watches patiently to make sure I see this through.

"Hello?" Roban answers.

Alice is mouthing the words *speaker phone*, which I try to ignore until she steps toward me. So, I do what I'm told.

"Hi, Roban. Is this a bad time?" I say.

"Nae. What's wrang? Ye soond upsit," he says, his words echoing down the tree lined street.

"Vanta ran away." My voice quivers and I know I'm not strong enough to tell him everything.

Alice whispers loudly, "Tell him about David!", but I swat her away like a pestering fly.

"Dae ye need me tae help look fur 'er? I'll drife doon thaur reit noo if that's whit ye need," he says.

"Yes! Please, Roban," I plead.

"Okay, I'll be reit thaur."

Alice is reaching for the phone so I quickly hang up and stuff my phone back in my dress pocket.

"You fucking liar." Alice's voice is full of scorn. "If you don't tell him, I will."

I don't know why I'm afraid to tell Roban what happened. It's not like I kissed David back. Maybe I want Roban to like David. Maybe I'm afraid he'll get jealous and leave.

"I'll tell him," I lie. But I think Alice can tell that I'm lying because she storms back toward the house without saying a word.

I can't escape the feeling that I've let Alice down somehow. Maybe I was out of line when I accused her of hating David because she has a crush on me. Even if that were true, Alice has always wanted the best for me and I can always count on her to call me out on my bullshit. I know she is trying to help, but does Roban really have to know? We've barely even discussed my divorce. All he knows is that my ex-husband cheated on me, so all he'll think is that he's a cheater if I mention that David and I are talking again. He doesn't know David the way I know him. Granted, the way we got together was ethically questionable, but David was there for me when no one else was.

When my father died, my mother couldn't even look at me. Probably because I look so much like him. I think it pained her to see me, and perhaps that's why she packed up her things and moved to Moab. To get away from me. But while my mother abandoned me when I needed her most, David was there to help me through it with his usual clinical methods, at least until I got a new psychiatrist. For ten years, David supported me and helped me through my grief. That has to mean something. David did a bad thing, but maybe that was my fault. I don't think he's a bad person. I want Roban and Alice to see that.

Alice never liked David. When I told her that I was romantically involved with my psychiatrist, she wanted to put a stop to it immediately. Every dinner together, every birthday, she was there to bust his balls. She didn't even pretend to like David for my sake. She simply said how she felt, loudly and unabashedly, until David and I sort of drifted away from her.

Still, I'm glad that Alice was there for me when I broke the news that we were getting divorced. She was ecstatic. If I recall, I was ecstatic, too. I guess I am happier now, without David. Maybe Alice is right and I should be more careful. I can't have David ruin the joy for which I fought so hard.

I circle the block looking for Vanta, but the sun is dipping below the horizon and the sky is getting dark. Soon, there will be no way I'll be able to see Vanta. All I can do now is head back home and hope that she reappears. What if she was on the porch right now and I've been out here looking for her like a damn fool? No, that can't be right. Alice would have called me if that were the case.

Alice. Oh no. I remember that Roban is on his way to the bungalow and Alice is there waiting for him. She's going to tell him everything! *Fuck.*

I quicken my pace and round the corner of the block, but I'm too late. I can see Roban's motorcycle parked by the curb.

I OPEN the front door slowly, as if I could possibly sneak in, but it's no use. Alice and Roban are sitting on the couch together. Their voices hush the moment I step inside. Roban shoots me this pained look and I know that Alice has already told him everything.

"I'll let you two talk," Alice says, rising from the couch and exiting the room. But first she raises her eyebrow at me. It feels like a challenge. A challenge for what, I don't know.

I take a seat next to Roban and set my hand on his knee. To my surprise, he doesn't shrink away. Instead, he sets his large, calloused hand on mine. I am comforted by its warmth.

"So," I say. I let out a little nervous chuckle. I didn't mean to do that. This is certainly no time for laughter, but I can't help it. Confrontation has always scared me and when I'm afraid I tend to smile or laugh. I really don't mean it. It usually irritates men to no end, but not Roban. His face remains stoic.

"Sae," he says. "Alice tauld me whit happened wi' yer ex-husbain."

"All of it?" I ask.

"Aw ay it."

"He kissed me, but it didn't mean anything," I say, but I'm talking so fast that my words are slurring together and I'm losing my train of thought. "I didn't kiss him back, it just happened so quickly, I—"

Roban presses his finger to my lips. "Ah believe ye," he says. "It micht nae hae meant anythin' tae ye, but ye can't pretend 'at it meant naethin' tae David. 'At it means naethin' tae me."

I look down, ashamed. "I'm sorry. I know this must seem silly, but I'd like to put this divorce behind us and try to be friends with him."

"He doesn't want tae be friends wi' ye. He wants ye back, Emily. Hoo am Ah supposed tae ignair 'at?"

"Listen. I'll talk to him about that. I'll make it clear that I don't want that kind of relationship with him anymore," I say. I almost convince myself, but clearly I can't convince Roban.

"Nae, Ah don't hink ye will," Roban sighs. "Thes bloke has ye wrapped aroond his finger. Ye need tae see heem fur whit he rilly is."

What does Roban think he is? Does he think he's an

abuser just like Alice does? Does he think of me like a victim?

"I think I'm stronger than you and Alice think I am," I say, retracting my hand from his knee. "You both see me as this brainwashed little girl, but I can stand up for myself."

"Recognizin' hoo he's hurt ye doesn't tak' awa' yer strength, Emily."

I ponder this for a moment. I want to argue with Roban, but it's difficult when he uses those damn words of his and says something that actually makes a lot of sense. David hurt me. Nobody is disputing that. But I hadn't considered that I could be hurt and tenacious at the same time. I don't know what to say. Fortunately, Roban always does.

"Ah ken ye want tae be thes independent woman, but ye can still be independent an' taken advantage ay. Alice an' Ah ur jist tryin' tae protect ye. Ye don't rilly need David, dae ye?"

"No," I pout. "You're right."

"'En why ur ye puttin' sae much energy intae defendin' th' man fa cheated oan ye?"

My face feels hot and I can tell there's this rage that's bubbling up inside of me. I can't tell if it's Roban that has upset me or David.

"Look, I really think he means well. He's offered to help with my mother and—"

"Dinnae accept help frae heem, Emily," Roban warns.

"Why not?"

"Coz that's hoo abusers lure in their victims. They pretend tae be braw an' helpful, but rilly they jist want tae gain control again," he says calmly. I, however, am getting very heated.

"Can you please stop using that word?" I wince.

"What word?"

"Abuser," I say. Even uttering the word leaves a foul taste in my mouth.

"But, Emily," Roban says, catching my hand, "That's whit he is. Ye micht nae see it 'at way yit, but one day, ye will. Ye see 'at he doesn't loove ye. Nae th' way Ah—" He stops. His icy blue eyes are staring directly into my own and his mouth is agape like he just said something he shouldn't have. "Whit Ah rilly mean is, ye shooldn't waste yer time oan someain that's bad fur ye."

I resist the urge to smile. Did Roban almost tell me he loves me?

"Okay," I say.

"Okay?"

"I'll try to see things from your perspective," I say. "But only because you love me."

Roban blinks at me, bewildered. "Ah didn't say—"

"You said enough." I lean forward and kiss him on the cheek.

Roban blushes underneath his thick beard.

While I said that I would listen to what he and Alice have been trying to tell me, I know that the second David comes through for me and finds a neurologist for my mother here, in Salt Lake City, I'll be indebted to him. Part of me still wants to be his friend, to impress him, to be there for him. But going back to him is out of the question. I have Roban and Alice and my mother, and I know I don't need David like I used to. I can only hope that I can be stronger the next time I see him. I need to set boundaries. That's always been my problem.

I don't mean to lie to Roban. In truth, this whole situation scares me, but then again, love always has.

fourteen

THE NEXT FEW weeks are great. I don't hear anything from David, I paint commissions during the day (some days I even paint for myself), and in the evenings I get to see Roban. Sometimes he spends the night, sometimes he doesn't. He's been really good about giving me my space, but we haven't broached the subject of love since he almost told me he loved me the night Vanta ran away. She's still missing. Poor thing. I wonder whether she is dead or alive, but no matter what, I just end up feeling like a terrible pet owner, like all of this is my fault for answering the door when David showed up. I'd say I try not to think about it, but it haunts me every waking moment. I want her to come home. I miss her warmth when she sleeps on the corner of the bed, the gentle sound of her purring once I climb under the covers. I miss her sitting on the windowsill while I paint in the morning. A piece of me is missing, and it's unfortunate that I didn't realize that it was even a part of myself until it was gone.

Luckily, when Roban sleeps over I don't feel so lonely. Still, there is this nagging thought that maybe he is here too much. Sometimes I just need a day to myself without exhausting myself with social obligations. Admittedly, things are easy with Roban, but I still feel like I need to make an effort to be interesting and entertaining. I don't want him to get bored of me. I want to be the type of person that does fun things all of the time, but I know that's not who I really am. I'm the type of person that wakes up early to drink their coffee in the dark with the fireplace burning. I'm the type of person that loves what they do so much that they spend almost every waking moment working. And then when I sufficiently exhaust myself, I like to lie down and read a book or scroll through social media. I've never been a fun person. I wonder how long I will have to pretend that I am.

IT'S SATURDAY, which means I try not to paint. Instead, I devote my weekends to spending time with Roban. However, tonight I don't have to entertain him. It's the other way around. Roban has invited me to a barbecue at his house in Glendale. His roommate, Matt, will be there. I'm sure he is less than pleased that I will be coming, but I think I can handle his attitude for an evening.

It's weird. We don't usually go to Roban's house. Probably because Matt is so standoffish. But tonight, not only will I get to try to woo Matt, but I will also get to meet Roban's other friends. Honestly, I'm amazed he has so many considering he has lived here for less than a year. I've lived here my entire life and Alice is my only friend. Roban is friendlier than me though. I don't know, maybe I just give off this bitchy vibe. Roban is like a puppy. He smiles constantly, and everyone likes having him around. He is an unmistakably positive force. Even Alice, who hates nearly everyone, liked him from the moment she saw him working in our yard, and her opinion means the world to me.

It's already late afternoon and I have just been lounging in my pajamas all day. I desperately need something to wear. I rummage through my closet, but it seems like all I own are bright patterned dresses with paint stains all over them and t-shirts with overalls of varying lengths. At least my black overall shorts don't have paint on them. They are fairly new, so I haven't managed to destroy them yet. I pick out a yellow and white striped crop top to wear underneath the overalls. This will have to do. *It's just a barbecue,* I think to myself. It's not like a black tie event. There will be nothing but men in ripped cargo shorts and baseball caps, drinking Miller Lite and eating burgers. I don't know why I am so concerned with impressing these people with my clothes. I don't know why I am suddenly so ashamed of my wardrobe.

I am supposed to be at Roban's house in thirty minutes. It takes twenty minutes to drive there, so I figure I will put on as much makeup as I can muster in ten minutes. Tinted moisturizer. Blush. Mascara. Red lipstick. Good enough. I grab my keys and race out the door. It's rude to be late.

"EMILY!" Roban calls as I open the gate to their backyard. He greets me with a kiss, much to the distaste of Matt who is manning the grill. "Come wi' me, Ah want ye tae meit everyone."

Roban takes my hand and leads me to a small group of men. At least one of them is wearing ripped cargo shorts. It turns out I was right about one thing.

"This must be Roban's new girlfriend!" one of them says, clapping Roban on the back.

"Yeah, isn't she somethin'," Roban says. He ruffles my hair a little bit in jest, but I am not laughing. I am not even smiling. Roban and I haven't talked about this. This man just called me his girlfriend in front of everyone, and Roban didn't push back on it at all. Is this how we become official? With zero conversation, just riding the assumptions of some guy in a backwards Utah Jazz cap with the stickers still on it? I wipe the sweat from my forehead. This is going to be worse than I imagined.

The man in the Jazz cap stretches out his hand to shake mine. Reluctantly, I give it to him, but I feel like by doing so, I am agreeing to be Roban's girlfriend. I don't think I'm ready for that.

"My name is Emily," I muster. I want to remind all of them that I do have a name. I am more than just "Roban's girlfriend." Oh great, now they've got me saying it. *I'm not his girlfriend. I'm not his girlfriend.*

"I'm Chris," he says gesturing to the other men standing in a circle, "And this is Josh, Nick, Ryan, and Michael."

"Nice to meet all of you," I say shyly. It's a bit overwhelming being the only woman here. Why aren't there other women here?

"So, Emily, what do you do?" Chris asks.

I open my mouth to speak but Roban answers for me.

"Mainly, she jist puts up wi' me," he laughs. There he goes again. Denying me my unique identity.

I guess I should just shut up and be Roban's girlfriend for the night, but the thought fills me with rage, so I clear my throat to cut through the men's laughter before announcing proudly, "Actually, I'm a painter." There is some residual laughter. It seems I'm still not being taken seriously.

"Can Ah gie ye a beer?" Roban asks.

"Please," I sigh. I take a moment to unclench my jaw.

Roban leaves me in the circle of men while he departs to grab us some beverages. I smile sheepishly. I am surrounded by wolves.

"So, what do you really do?" says Ryan. "Like, for money?"

"That's kind of a rude question, don't you think?" I blurt out. With Roban gone, my filter disappears.

"Well, I just mean, you can't really make a living as an artist," Michael chimes in, defending Ryan. "He's just trying to get to know you since your Roban's girlfriend and all."

I want to scream. "Why can't I make a living as an artist?"

"You know, the whole starving artist thing. Who would pay for a painting anyway?" Michael says. The men all laugh in unison.

"Lots of people do," I say flatly, "In fact, I just got a three-thousand dollar check for a portrait I was commissioned to do online."

The laughter stops and Josh gasps. "Three thousand dollars? For a painting?"

"Yes, does that surprise you?"

"It does, actually," says Josh. "So are you famous or something?"

"No," I say, "I'm just good at what I do."

The men look uncomfortable. I'm glad I was able to make them feel as unwelcome as I do.

The conversation stops and the men break apart, heading toward Matt and the grill and leaving me behind. I don't follow. I just wait for Roban to return from inside the house with my drink. For a brief moment, I consider shocking all of them and shotgunning the whole beer. Partly because I want them to think I am cool, but mostly because I want to stifle the animosity I feel toward Roban's friends. Who keeps company like this anyway?

Just as I pull out my phone to text Alice, I hear the back door to the house bang shut. Roban is approaching with two beers in coozies. He hands me the purple one. It's a Coors, but the stereotype still remains. Roban begins walking toward the men by the grill, but I don't step forward with him.

"Roban," I say, but he must not hear me because he's already gone. I feel weak. Why can't I be stronger when he is around?

I can't bear to be around those guys a second longer, but I can't bring myself to leave. Instead, I take a seat on a bench next to a planter filled with herbs. The smell of rosemary is suffocating.

I take out my phone and begin composing a text for Alice when my phone buzzes and I get a notification. I am astonished to see that the notification is a text from David:

Hey. Hope you are well. I just wanted to check in and see if you've found the cat yet. I still feel terrible about that. How's your mom? xx

My heart leaps. I had actually been wondering if and when I would hear from him again. I'm glad he reached out. I am desperate to talk to anybody.

My mom says she's fine, I write, *but I am thinking about making another trip to visit her just to be sure. Vanta is still missing.*

Send. David's response is instantaneous.

Do you need some company for the drive to Moab? ;)

He's flirting with me again. I don't know how to handle

it. I figure now is as good of a time as ever to tell him about Roban, seeing as I am apparently his girlfriend now. The thought still makes me restless and itchy.

No, but thanks for the offer. I'm actually seeing someone.

Send. I worry that by saying this that I have eliminated any chance of David finding a neurologist for my mother in Salt Lake. I panic and change the subject, reminding him of his offer.

Any word on finding a doctor for my mom?

No response. I stare at my phone, blocking out the sound of Roban's friends' laughter in the background. *Please respond,* I think over and over again. It's like a prayer that gets no answer.

My pleading thoughts are interrupted by Roban, whose hand startles me by resting on my back. He takes a seat beside me. I stuff my phone in my pocket. It feels like I'm keeping a secret.

"Is everythin' okay?" he says. His eyes soften toward me. How can someone so gentle and considerate be friends with those assholes?

"Fine," I say. The word catches in my throat. "I'm fine."

"Wa don't ye come ower an' gab wi' th' guys?" he asks.

"I'm fine right here," I protest. I don't want to seem overly dramatic, so I figure it's best that the words I exchanged with his friends remain unsaid. Roban really seems to like these guys. I don't know how close they really are, but I would hate for their friendship to end because I was being too sensitive. "You go on. Don't worry about me."

But really, I do want him to worry about me. I want to make a scene. I want to throw my beer at Josh's head. But I don't do any of these things. I play the role of patient, cool-headed girlfriend.

"Ur ye sure?" Roban asks again. God, he is relentless.

"I'm sure."

"Umm, if ye say sae. Dae ye want cheese oan yer burger?"

"Sure," I say. It doesn't matter to me. By the time it's ready, I will be long gone.

My phone buzzes. I nearly drop my phone as I rapidly withdraw it from my pocket. It's a response from David.

I was afraid that was the case. But listen, I am willing to fight for you. We really had something, didn't we?

He ignored the question about finding a doctor entirely. He really is hellbent on getting me back. I look up at the men circling the grill, talking loudly and proudly and laughing in regular, appropriate intermissions at each of their anecdotes. *David was never like this,* I think to myself. I almost wish I didn't have the thought, but then I consider it for a moment. Was I happy with David? No. No. Of course not. That is silly of me to even consider.

This whole situation has me dizzy with despair. I don't know if I love Roban. I don't know if I ever loved David. I don't know if I am capable of love at all. It's too hard, always being *on* for someone, pretending to like their friends, pretending like everything is okay when all I can think about is my mortgage and my sick mother. Maybe some women aren't meant to do it all. It seems to me that a woman can be happy, in a relationship, or successful in her career, but never all three at once. You can only pick two, at most. Most of us can only pick one. Which one will I pick?

My thoughts are once again interrupted by the sound of the men's laughter. God, they are so annoying. Why am I even here? Clearly these guys are single because there isn't another woman here. I can hazard a guess as to why they are in their mid-thirties and still alone. Who would put up with that? Why does Roban? Maybe I don't know him as well as I thought I did.

I decide to chug the rest of my beer. It is quite full, but I suck down every last drop anyway. I can't be here anymore. I need to leave.

Hastily, I pull out my keys and try to sneak to the back gate. The guys are so preoccupied that I doubt they would even notice that I am gone. The gate creaks loudly as I open it and when I turn around, everyone is looking at me—including Roban. They each look surprised, as if my leaving was ever in question after how they treated me when Roban wasn't around.

"Sorry," I whisper. I can feel my eyes pooling with water, and a single tear drips down my cheek. I turn and exit the gate, leaving Roban and his friends behind.

I quickly get in my car and put the key in the ignition. I can see Roban closing the gate, coming after me, but I put the car in drive and speed off, ignoring the fact that Roban is standing alone in the street in my rearview mirror.

I know what I need to do. It's hard, but it's necessary. Yes, a woman can be happy, in a relationship, or successful in her career, but never all three at once. I have made my choice.

fifteen

IT'S LATE when Roban shows up at the bungalow. His texts and phone calls were all ignored, so it was only a matter of time before he decided to drive up to the house and knock on the door. His knocks are panicked and frequent. I think briefly of ignoring him at the door, but I know I need to confront him. Unfortunately, I've never been one for confrontation.

I turn the locks on the door and pull it open. It sticks a little, still swollen from the heat.

"Emily," Roban says, exasperated. He pulls me into a tight hug. Normally, I would be comforted by his touch, but instead, I recoil, wriggling free of his grasp. "Whit is wrang wi' ye? Dae ye ken hoo rude it was fur ye tae leave withit sae much as a goodbye? Th' guys—"

"*I'm* rude?" I say in disbelief. "Oh, don't get me started on those friends of yours!"

Roban's brow furrows. He seems angry. I've never seen him angry before.

"Ah need ye tae talk tae me, Emily. Ye can't jist leave loch 'at."

"And I suppose you are in charge of what I can and cannot do, is that right? Now that we're boyfriend and girlfriend?" My voice is sour and venomous, but I cannot bite my tongue.

"We are... boyfriend an' girlfriend. Aren't we?" Roban asks. His face tenses up.

I had a lot of time to think about this on the drive home. It's hard to say the words I rehearsed now with Roban in front of me, but I have to do this.

"No, Roban," I say with finality. "We're not."

Roban's face turns white. His icy blue eyes are glossy and his lip trembles as he tries to speak. Over and over, he opens his mouth to say something, but he touches his fist to his mouth and avoids my gaze, blinking back tears.

"Ah—Ah—" he stammers, "I'm sorry. Ah must hae misreid everythin'."

I want to comfort him. It breaks me to see him like this, but I have made my decision. I need to follow through with it, and quickly, before I back out entirely. Why does standing up for myself have to be so damn uncomfortable?

"You can't just presume that I am your girlfriend, Roban. We have to talk about that sort of thing. You can't just wake up one day and decide, yes, I'm your girlfriend. That's not how things work!"

"Yoo're reit. We hae tae communicate," Roban agrees. "But Ah rilly thooght ye liked me."

"I do like you!" I plead, "But things just aren't going the way they should."

Roban's face twists into a look of puzzlement. "Whit dae ye mean?"

Where do I even begin? All those thoughts I had, all those words I conjured, evade me now. I try to muster up some courage.

"Roban," I say, rubbing my forehead, "Remember when I told you I would date you under some conditions? I told you that I need my space, that I need to be your second priority because you will never be my first. And I know you told me that you just wanted to spend time with me, and I have tried to honor that to my detriment, but you need something else to occupy your time. I have a lot going on all of the time. I'm just not sure I have time for... you."

I struggle to get that last word out. I didn't realize that I held these beliefs until I actually voiced them. I feel terrible, but I needed to say it.

Roban's eyes widen. "Whaur is thes comin' frae? Ah thooght ye waur happy?"

"I was. I am. I just—" I take a deep breath. "I just think that maybe I would be better off alone."

Silence follows. Roban and I stare at each other in a standoff, waiting for who will speak first.

"Sae thes is it," Roban says. He's choking a little, gasping for air, but manages the words, "We're dain 'en?"

I think about my next words carefully. If I say yes, this really is it. I lose Roban forever. Gentle, caring, poet, Roban. But also, clingy and presumptuous, and that's the part I can't handle. This summer has been great, but I can't ignore this sneaking suspicion that I would be happier by myself. I am still recovering from my divorce, for Christ's sake. Things are clearly unresolved with David, not that he is factoring into this, and I need to focus on my mother and my art. That is what is important right now. Not gallivanting about the city with a brawny Scotsman. It was fun while it lasted, but I feel this relationship closing before me.

"Yes," I say. "We're done."

Roban's tears are coating his cheeks, seeping into his beard, making the dark brown hairs sparkle in the twilight.

He is beautiful even when he is sad. It pains me to do this to him, it really does. If I were ready to give myself, all of myself, to someone, I'd want it to be him. Seeing him broken like this makes me feel like maybe I've made a huge mistake.

"Goodbye then, lass," he says, turning around and beginning his descent down the wooden porch steps. "Ah wish ye weel. Ah rilly dae."

Roban walks off into the darkness, with only the street-lights catching his large, sullen silhouette.

I CLOSE the door softly and collapse upon the floor. I thought that I would feel better breaking up with Roban, but instead I feel so much worse. For some reason, I thought I might feel relieved, the way I did the night I discovered David's infidelity and told him that I wanted a divorce. Roban, it seems, is nothing like David. But I already knew that.

Alice must have heard me crying because she appears in the doorway leading to the kitchen, gently rapping on the archway.

"Emily..." she says softly, "Is everything okay? What happened?"

I can't stop sobbing long enough to get the words out. I try and I try, but the break up seems even more real when I try to utter it aloud, bring it into existence.

"Did something happen at the barbecue?" Alice asks. She sits down on the floor next to me and rubs my back with the care and tenderness that only a family member or a close friend can. I bury my face in her shoulder and she wraps her arms around me.

"I broke up with Roban," I wail.

"Babe," Alice whispers, "Why did you do that? You were so happy!"

I cry even harder and Alice simply strokes my hair and pulls me closer, all the while cooing, "Shh... shh... it's going to be all right."

"Did I make a huge mistake?" I blink up at her.

"Only you can know that," she says.

"I just—I don't know what I want," I whimper. "I thought I was happy, but something just seemed off. I just want to be independent. Is that too much to ask?"

Alice looks down at me, such kindness in her eyes. "It's not, but babe, you were already there. Ever since your divorce, I've been in awe of you and your strength. You're fucking killing it with your painting right now. Did Roban really interfere with that?"

"I shouldn't need a man to be happy," I say stubbornly.

"No," she says, "You're right. You shouldn't and you don't. But it's not a weakness if you find happiness in other people. It just makes you...well, human."

"How do you do it?"

Alice laughs, "Who said I am happy?"

This shocks me. Alice has always seemed so happy, so independent, so free. Was I wrong about that, too?

"Aren't you?" I say, "You've got a fulfilling career, you've got your book. What else could you ask for?"

"Sometimes joy in life isn't about what you want, but what you need. I need companionship, same as you. People aren't meant to be alone, Emily. We're always better off when we are surrounded by people that love us. Not just platonic love, but real, tangible, romantic love."

"But how do you know if you've got it right?" I ask.

Alice mulls this over. I can see the gears in her head

turning. Then she says, "I'm not certain that you ever know for sure. It takes faith. You have to believe in forces greater than yourself. I'm probably the wrong person to be asking considering my love life is just one tragedy after another, but I like to think that when you know things are right, you'll feel it."

I don't know if I felt it with Roban. I don't know if I felt it with David. As far as I'm concerned, I don't know what I'm feeling ninety-nine percent of the time. How do I know whether I loved Roban or if I was just riding the high that comes with all new relationships. The problem is I can't trust myself.

"Thanks, Alice," I say, rising to my feet. I wipe my damp face with the collar of my striped shirt. "I think I just need to be alone for a while."

"Okay," she says. Her face is a knot of concern. "I'm here if you need me."

I shut myself in my bedroom, locking the door behind me. I don't need any more wisdom from Alice tonight. It's just making the waters murkier than before. Things were fine with Roban, right? I felt good, honestly. Better than I did before we met. But I don't know, something just felt... off. I can't pinpoint when I started feeling it, but something was telling me to run. Maybe I'm just scared of what it means to really love someone.

I climb under the covers on my bed and pull the sheet over my head, just wishing that all of this would magically resolve itself. I wish I knew what it meant to be happy. God, I need to go back to therapy. I think about texting my psychiatrist, to see if I can get an appointment tomorrow so we can sort this out, but it's late. I wouldn't hear back from her tonight. David on the other hand... David is probably awake.

I take out my phone and begin composing a text message.

Can you talk?

I tap send. I hold my phone close to my chest, waiting, praying for a vibration. I wait and wait until my eyes close and I begin drifting off to sleep. Just as things are about to go black, my tranquility is interrupted by the incessant buzzing of my phone on the bed beside me.

I groan and think about ignoring it, until it dawns on me that it's probably David. I'm the one who reached out to him. I should probably take this.

I look at the clock. It's two in the morning and sure enough, David's name is flashing on my screen. I sit up and slide to answer the call.

"David?" I say. There is sleep in my voice, so I have to clear my throat.

"Emily. You're okay, right?"

There it is. That loaded question. My entire life, every time someone has asked me if I am okay, I get that familiar pain in the back of my throat that I get when I'm about to cry. The pain of repressed emotion. The pain of sadness welling up inside me. It's as if by asking this question that it dawns on me that I am not okay, I have never been okay, and I will probably never be okay. I hate to be reminded.

This time is no different.

"No," I say, swallowing back the pain like a large pill. "I need to talk to someone."

"Don't you have Alice? Or that guy you've been seeing?"

David sounds a little bitter. There's an attitude, an edge to his voice, that cuts me every time.

"I broke up with him," I manage, but the lump in my throat is persistent. I decide to release the pressure building up and let the tears fall.

David doesn't respond to what I've told him. There's just silence on the other end. For a moment, I think I've lost him.

"David? Hello?"

"That's interesting," he says finally. "I'm sorry to hear that." He says he's sorry, but deep down I know he's never been sorry for anything in his life. He is probably thrilled by the news. "What can I do to help?"

"I don't know," I say, "We were married for ten years. You probably know me better than I know myself. Am I incapable of love?"

"No," David says, "If there is one thing I know about you, it's that you are full of nothing but love."

"Wasn't there a bit of hatred in there, too?" I ask. Surely, there must have been. Being married to David was like tensing my shoulders for a decade. The moment I found the belly button ring in our bed, it's like I was finally able to release that tension. But maybe he's right. Maybe I really did love him. Why else would I be talking to him at two o'clock in the morning?

"Hatred?" David scoffs. "Maybe a little. You're a fire-cracker though! A little bit of animosity toward the world is natural. I'll admit, I deserved a fair share of it."

I laugh. It's nice that we can joke about this now.

"Why did you do it?" I ask.

"Why did I do what?"

He's oblivious.

"Why did you cheat on me?"

David coughs. "I honestly have no idea, Emily."

Is he serious? He has no idea? Nobody cheats for no reason. I wish he would tell me that he loved another woman, that I made him miserable, that he wanted to hurt me, that it was a mistake made in the throes of passion. Anything.

"Why do we hurt the people we love?" I say. I'm beginning to think I'm more like David than I thought.

"I can't say I have an answer to that either. But you can't be too hard on yourself. You did what you had to do, right?"

"Right," I say reluctantly. "At least, I think I did."

"Listen," David says, "You want to know why we do the things we do? Put simply, it's because we want to. We desire an outcome and we make it happen. We are in charge of our own destinies. You're just controlling your own."

"I guess that makes sense," I say. "But does that excuse the way we treat other people? I've got to say, I feel really bad about everything."

"You are a goddess, Emily. You can do whatever you want to get whatever you want."

I'm flattered, but it doesn't feel right. I don't think I get a free pass to just steamroll over everyone because I want to be this big shot artist. I've always believed that everyone deserves kindness, dignity, and respect. Maybe it's weak of me to think so. It's strange, but I feel like maybe I can be stronger with David's guidance.

"Do you want to grab drinks sometime?" I ask.

"Just name the time and place. I'll be there," David says.

"Thanks for talking to me. I really needed it."

"Of course," he says. "I hope I helped. I'll see you soon."

I hang up the phone and set it face down on my bedside table. I don't know if I feel better necessarily, but I certainly feel less guilty. But I think David was wrong about one thing. I don't believe I am capable of love. I think it's just rancor that fuels me. How else could I be so careless with Roban's heart?

sixteen

THE DAYS after the breakup are difficult. I could scarcely get out of bed. I just cried and slept all day, and for what? *I* am the one that broke up with Roban. I thought I had a good reason, too. My days, which I will admit were mostly filled with painting, revolved around seeing Roban, and without spontaneity, without whimsy, each day blurred into the next until all I could remember was spending time with him. What happened to my ambitions? What was happening with my art? More importantly, what was happening with my mother's health and her boyfriend, Robert? All of these things were dwarfed by my relationship with Roban. It was only a matter of time until I snapped.

I thought I would feel relief, but now all I can feel is this nagging sense of regret. With my evenings open to do as I please, I find myself not wanting to do anything—just soak in the loneliness that envelops me. Late nights, when I finally crawl into bed, I am reminded of the way Roban used to run his hands down the length of my body, how he would smooth my messy hair out of my face and kiss me softly, first on the lips and then my cheek, my neck, my collarbone. Then I am shocked back into reality. The darkness is thick and heavy. Sometimes I pick up my phone and think about texting Roban, apologizing, and asking for him to come back. But then I end up texting David instead, as if that will give me strength and resolve in my decisions. Then the morning comes and I am once again filled with regret.

The worst part is that it is affecting my art. Even now, as I paint small strokes of different shades of black (violet-black, blue-black, green-black, etc.), I realize that I am changed. My work had never been this bleak. Over and over, I keep attempting the same painting: one that best represents the inky static that falls over me at night when I am most lonely. But I can't capture it. My ability to translate the bodiless and ethereal to something corporeal and tactile is lost, possibly because my own ability to identify my emotions is compromised.

I decide to scrap the canvas once again, sanding off hours of work and coating it with white primer, when I hear light steps creaking the floorboards behind me. For a brief moment, I think it might be Roban roused from his sleep.

"Alice!" I gasp, "You scared me! I thought you might have been—"

"A ghost?" she says.

"Something like that," I mumble. "What's going on? Why are you just standing there like that?"

She is leaning on the archway of the dining room (a.k.a. my painting room) holding a cup of fresh coffee. Her eyes are soft and drooping, dark circles under her eyes—or maybe that's just a shadow.

"I'm concerned about you," she says.

"Why? I am totally fine," I lie.

Alice squints at me, giving my body a glance. She looks like she is trying to decipher a puzzle.

"No, you are not. I see it every day, Emily. You can say that you're miserable. I won't judge you."

The paint brush in my hand begins to tremble. I am vibrating with remorse. But how do I tell her that? If I say I've made a mistake, she'll just insert herself into the situation like she always does.

"No, really. I'm fine," I say.

"Emily, you're shaking."

Alice sets down her coffee cup on the floor and slowly approaches me, like I'm a broken bird that she wants to save but she's trying not to frighten it. This gesture destroys my casual, carefree facade. Piece by piece it comes crumbling down until I am exposed. Tears swell up in the corners of my eyes and I throw myself into Alice's arms, sobbing.

"It's okay," she says. "Shh... Everything is going to be okay."

There are no words. Alice already knows what is wrong. Not that I could ever make out the words anyway. Admitting my feelings aloud would be admitting defeat.

"You miss Roban, don't you?" she coos. She rubs my back gently, as if she were comforting a child. I simply nod. I still can't bring myself to utter the words. "Emily, you're so stupid." Alice chuckles, which makes me stifle a laugh through my tears.

"Have I made a huge mistake?" I ask. I know the answer, but I want to hear it.

"That's impossible for me to know," Alice says. "Do *you* think you've made a mistake?"

Thinking about it just makes the tears fall faster, my breathing more interrupted by sharp, intermittent inhalations. I release myself from Alice's embrace and pick up the paint brush coated in white, once more turning toward the canvas.

"I can't get anything right," I say. "Not with Roban, not with my mom, and not with this fucking painting."

I slap more primer on the canvas, angrily brushing it over the remains of dark paint below. I'm ready to try again, at least for the catharsis if not the feeling of productivity. I have to keep my mind occupied or I'll start crying again.

"Emily, calm down. It's going to be okay," Alice says.

"How? How can you possibly know that?" I snarl.

"Because no matter what happens, with Roban or with your mom or with your art, you are resilient. You'll find a way to cope."

"And what if I don't?" I say.

"Trust that you will, and you will."

I turn my back to Alice. I need concrete answers, not my best friend parroting years of self-help books.

"That sounds nice and all," I say, "But that doesn't help me right now."

Alice is never one to back down or walk away. She'll argue her point until it's lost all meaning, so long as she is deemed right in the end.

"Sometimes things just suck. If you won't admit it, I will: Right now, your life is shit. But that doesn't mean it will always be shit. Do you see what I'm saying?" She pauses, but I have no reply. I am steadily covering the canvas in primer, trying to block out her words to no avail. "Tomorrow is another day. Things could always turn around, and it's in your power to make it happen. You are in control of your future, Emily. Don't lose sight of that."

"Jesus, Alice. I am so sick of hearing that I'm in control of how I feel. I'm not. I can't control how I feel, and I don't know what I am feeling half of the time. All I know now is that I feel bad. And I will continue to feel bad until I figure out why. I can't change anything if I don't know *what* to change."

Alice sets her hand on my shoulder, stilling my arm from its task. I turn and look at her.

"We'll figure it out," she says softly. "Together."

"You're a better friend than I deserve."

"Everyone deserves a friend." She throws me a wink. "But you're right. I'm a pretty good one."

She makes her way out of the dining room and picks her mug up off the floor.

"And she's humble, too!" I call out. She laughs as she disappears back into the kitchen.

The canvas is nearly done being primed for yet another attempt to convey how I feel. But I'm not ready to try again today. One failed attempt is enough for now. I stare at the blank canvas though and try to imagine what my feelings would look like if they were able to course through my paint brush. I was right with the shades of black. There are so many shades of darkness within me. How else did I find myself in this predicament? But Alice reminded me that there are lighter shades, too. There is hope that tomorrow will be a better day, but I have to take steps to make it so. With darkness, there is light. With light, there is darkness. One cannot exist without the other. It was my mistake forgetting that.

I spend most of the day in bed. Not doing anything in particular. Just staring at the walls and thinking. I am too tired, too distracted, to do anything else. I do discover one thing though: I am alone, and I will be alone forever if I don't get over myself. But how do I retain my freedom if I belong to someone else? Perhaps I am thinking about it all wrong. Maybe being with someone is not the same as belonging to them. Maybe love is still in the realm of possibility.

I take out my phone, my thumb hovering over the call button with Roban's name beside it, but I can't do it. I close the app and lock my phone again, setting it beside me on the bed. I know what I should do, but I can't bring myself to do it. Something is holding me back.

I want to call Roban. I know that I should. But it's like I'm not even in control of my body as I pick up my phone again and scroll down to David's name. I think about calling him, too, but I hesitate. Why is turning to David any different than relying on Roban? I think that maybe letting David back into my life has left me confused. But I need him, don't I? Or rather, my mother needs him and his connections. He has yet to confirm whether he has actually talked to a neurologist. I'm eager for this to be over, for David to find the right doctor so I can focus on getting my mother back to Salt Lake City so I can take care of her. I want to nag him about it, but he's never responded well to my nagging before. This time wouldn't be any different.

Frustrated, I get out of bed and walk out to the front porch. The afternoon sun is beating down on the yard, but there is a slight chill in the breeze—a promise of the autumn to come. The wind tickles the leaves on the chokecherry sapling, which has grown a bit since Roban planted it earlier this summer. Even the yuccas, which were babies themselves, seem to be growing in size, but it will be years before they are fully mature. Roban and his crew did a really good job on the yard. It's so much better than the dying lawn that David insisted on keeping during our ten years of marriage. I begged him and begged him to let it die, to replace it with something that requires less maintenance, but my ideas were always shot down.

It wasn't just my ideas about the yard that were rebuffed. My thoughts on livening up the house, giving it some character, were constantly rejected. David liked his corporate-looking arm chairs and grey walls. I wanted antique furniture and throw pillows in wild colors. I wanted to hang my art in the house, but David said no. He said he didn't understand it and that most of my paintings made him uncomfortable. He must have sensed how many of those paintings I did when I was upset with him, or rather when he was upset with me. There was a subtle violence in my work back then. It's only now that I am really finding my unique style: vivid, playful, happy. I realize that could be why I am struggling so much to capture the darkness in me. That's just not who I am. Perhaps Roban had a hand in that.

As I ponder this—where I've been and where I'm going—I hear a peculiar sound. It's small and squeaky, but it is unmistakably familiar. I look around the yard, searching for the source, but there is nothing there but plants and rocks. I hear it again, the squeak. It's coming from right behind me.

I turn around quickly and see a little black cat pawing at the door.

"Vanta?" I say aloud.

The cat mews again, louder now that I am looking at its golden eyes. There is no mistake. This is definitely Vanta. She's a bit bigger now and her hair is longer and fluffier than when I last saw her, but she is back and she wants to come inside.

I pick her up and cradle her in my arms like a baby, the way I used to before she escaped. She gives me a cautionary scratch, so I set her down and open the door for her. She walks inside. It's as if she was never gone.

I follow her inside and get her some food and water. I don't know what she has been through these past few weeks, but I hope that she found what she needed to survive. She approaches the food dish immediately. As she eats, I can't resist crouching down on the hard tile kitchen floor and petting her. She purrs as she devours each bit of kibble.

"You must have been hungry," I say, scratching down her spine. She stops eating for a moment to arch her back and look up at the ceiling. It's as if she hasn't been pet the whole time she was gone. Clearly content, it's like she is remembering what it's like to be home.

I leave her alone to finish eating, just watching her in awe. I can't believe she is back. My first impulse is to text Roban and let him know she's been found. Then Alice. Then David. Instead, I choose to sit with her for a moment, observe her, and make sure she is okay. She's a little dirty, but I don't see any wounds. She seems... happy? Watching her now after missing her so much for so long, I realize that I *do* love her. I guess she just had to disappear to make me see it. It's true what they say: absence makes the heart grow fonder.

I think I've got love all wrong. Love is not controlling. Love is not possession. Love is caring about someone or something so much that it consumes you, and there is nothing wrong with being consumed by it. In time, you see that it brings you comfort and happiness. My loving Vanta doesn't mean I want to possess her. I just want her around. There it is: I just want her around.

I understand what Roban has been trying to tell me. He just wanted me around, and I was so stupid to run away from that, to be absent all of the time. I can still have everything I want for myself and be present for someone that cares for me as deeply as Roban does, right? Surely I can be an artist, a caretaker, and a girlfriend all simultaneously. One shouldn't take away from the others.

Vanta finishes her kibble, licks her lips, and nudges my hand with her face. Taking the cue, I pet her head and scratch her cheeks. A little grimace appears. She loves this. She loves me. And even though she ran away, she came back because she knew that her place was here, with me.

It dawns on me that my love for Vanta does not take away her independence. She is free to do as she pleases, and when she is ready, she'll come to me to reciprocate. I can't make her do anything. I can't make her love me in return. But she does, in her own weird way. It's really as simple as that.

seventeen

I DON'T KNOW why I am getting so dressed up. This is David we're talking about here. He's seen me at my worst, but as always, I feel compelled to look my best. A tight green dress hugs my curves, with only a few inches of fabric covering my backside. I can't even remember why I own this dress. I never wear things like this. I much prefer loose, flowing garments, but ever since I broke things off with Roban, I haven't had the energy to wash a load of laundry, and so this form-fitting green dress is the only acceptable thing that remains in my closet. I worry what David will say when he sees me. *Why are you wearing that? Do you know what men think about women who dress like that? Seriously, you should go home and change.* Is it all in my head, or did he really used to say things like that? My memory must be faulty.

I call a Lyft to the bar. It's this little speakeasy in the center of Sugar House. The inside casts an orange glow from the vintage Edison bulbs hanging from the ceiling and on the sconces on the walls. The walls are lined with tables and lounges. I see one empty two-top and go take a seat there, my seat facing the door. Despite having lived in Sugar House for the last decade, I have only been to this bar once for David's birthday. It's just not my scene. Everything is just so... David. They exclusively play jazz music, and not the soft kind with tender piano melodies, but rather the kind with excessive horns and no discernible rhythm. It drives me crazy, but David said he wanted to meet here. I would have much preferred the Irish pub that the college kids don't seem to know about. Everyone here is so well-dressed. The men remind me of Christian Bale in *American Psycho*. Seriously, who comes to a place like this to have fun?

I don't grab a drink yet. I'm too nervous and I'm afraid that if I start before he gets here I'll just get sloppy and he will reprimand me for that, too. It's best to stay sober until he arrives.

I get out my phone and stare at it in case he calls, but really I'm waiting for Roban to reach out. It seems odd that he hasn't. He used to always text me when we were apart. I rarely responded right away, but now I'm wishing I had. He deserved better than that.

I feel a shadow over me, like someone is hovering. It's not until I hear them clearing their throat that I notice that David has arrived and he is standing with two drinks beside me.

"Oh, sorry," I say, stuffing my phone back in my purse. "Hi, David."

He sets the drinks on the table and opens his arms wide for a hug. I oblige him by rising from my seat and wrapping my arms gently around him. He pulls me in close and nuzzles his face into my hair. I let go first and return to my seat.

"Emily, you look..." David pauses.

"Yeah?" I'm nervous, bracing myself for his criticism.

"Amazing."

I sigh in relief. "Thanks."

There is an awkward pause. I am fiddling with the stem of my cocktail, condensation dripping onto my fingers, while David just stares. I look away. I don't like this. I don't like being watched by him. His eyes are piercing through me, and like a rush of blood to the head, all of the memories I have of our marriage begin flashing before me.

My eyes meet his and I find myself wanting to disappear. Why did I agree to this? Has David really changed at all?

"So you found your cat?" he says, breaking the silence.

"Yeah," I chuckle nervously, "She just appeared at the door and now she is safe and sound."

"That's great. And your mom, how is she doing?"

This feels like a job interview. There is an unusual amount of pressure in this conversation. I'm not sure if I can handle it.

"I haven't really talked to her lately. She is busy with her new boyfriend. You know how it is."

"Ah, so Linda found herself a man," David takes a large sip of his Scotch. "It's about time. I'm proud of her."

My face is hot and I can feel the blood pulsing in my veins. The urge to argue is too strong to resist. "What do you mean it's about time? She's been grieving."

"Calm down, I didn't mean anything by it," David says. "She's just better off with a man around to help her out now. That's all. It's good she's not grieving anymore."

"I'm sorry, but I think she's been getting along fine on her own," I say. I take a sip from the cocktail straw, but I'm biting it so hard that the tip breaks.

"Alright, alright. I didn't mean to offend. I forget how quick to anger you are."

More memories flood my brain. All of the fights, all of the crying, all of the blaming myself for our unhappiness. I want to convince myself that this is new behavior, but I know better. I know that he has been this way all along. I decide to brush it off. I'm not Angry Emily anymore. Instead, I remind myself of my purpose here. I change the subject.

"So, how is the doctor search going?"

"The doctor search?" David's left brow raises in confusion.

"For my mom?"

David takes another drink and nods his head after he's had a moment to think about it. "Oh yeah. Sorry. I haven't had time to look into that yet."

Rage consumes me now. There's an ache in my stomach and my shaking hands are starting to sweat. I hide them in my lap. I don't want my tremors to be misinterpreted. After all, David is always analyzing my behavior. He thinks I haven't noticed that about him, but it was something that came to light when I found a new psychiatrist. Once I picked up on it, I could never forget it.

"David," I say. I am completely fed up with his shit now. "Are you going to refer my mom to a neurologist or not? We don't have time to keep waiting on you."

His eyes are wide. He looks stunned. I've never spoken to him like this. Not since that night I discovered his infidelity.

"Look, I've just been busy. I care about you and Linda still. I'll take care of it."

I cup my forehead in my hands.

"I don't know why I came here. I thought I needed your help, but the truth is, I don't. We can find a neurologist here on our own. I doubt you have the connections anyway. You're a psychiatrist for God's sake."

I quickly chug the remaining half of my cocktail and get up to leave. David catches me by the wrist. His grip is so tight that it pulls me back to him.

"Emily." His tone has changed. "Why don't you sit down? You're not being rational. Come, sit."

"Don't use your psychiatrist voice on me, David. It doesn't work anymore." I break free from his grasp. "You are a manipulative, conniving bastard, always gaslighting me and making me feel like I'm the one who is out of control. But now I know that I've been in control this whole time. It just took getting away from you to realize it."

"What? So you think you're better off without me now because of Roban? Give me a break," David scoffs, "I gave you everything. You wouldn't be half the artist you are today if it weren't for me. If you ever amount to anything, I hope you know that it's because of me that you got there. But you won't. Not now. You'll never be anything more than a hobbyist."

I feel the sting on my palm before I even realize that I've slapped him. He's gripping his face and cowering in his chair as the entire bar looks at us.

"You don't know anything about me," I say and turn away, marching toward the door. I'm walking down the sidewalk outside where the cool air can fill my lungs and calm me down. I keep walking. I don't want David coming after me. I am grateful that I chose to wear flats, but as can be expected from a long walk home, they pinch at my skin, forming large blisters all over the tops of my feet. I don't pay them any mind. I just keep marching home.

THE FIRST THING I do the next morning is call my mother. It's been too long since we've spoken. She doesn't usually reach out to me, so it's not surprising that I haven't heard from her. But I should be better. She has Parkinson's, after all. I should be calling her every day.

"Mom?" I ask anxiously after the phone stops ringing.

"Emily, I'm so glad you called," she says. "How are things?"

Where do I begin? It's been so long. So much has happened. She never knew about Vanta running away, about David showing up, about my break up with Roban.

"Oh, Mom!" I start crying, blubbering over my words. "Everything is a mess! I've been talking to David and he said he could find you a good neurologist here in Salt Lake, but—but he was just using it as an excuse to get closer to me. He kissed me, Mom! And then I lost Roban. I—I don't know what to do."

"Oh, honey," my mother coos. "Calm down and start from the beginning."

I try to compose myself by taking deep breaths. Slowly, I begin to feel stable and I tell my mother everything. The words tumble out quickly, and I hope she is able to follow, but I can't stop speaking until I get everything out. Once the final thought exits my mouth, I pause and wait for her response.

"Well, it sounds like a lot. But sweetie, you can't blame yourself for what happened with David. He is a vile man and he took advantage of your kindness. You were right to stand up to him. As for me, I don't need a fancy neurologist. I'm getting perfectly fine care right where I am," she says. There's a stubbornness in her voice. I should have known she would never have come to Salt Lake City freely. There are too many memories here, and she has successfully evaded them for years.

"Are you sure?" I say. "I could always have Alice move out and you could have the spare bedroom. It wouldn't be any trouble at all. Really."

"I'm sure. Now, what are you going to do about Roban?"

I start crying again, softer now, but the sadness consumes me all the same.

"I think I've messed things up too much, Mom. It's too late."

"How do you know that?" she says. "Did Roban tell you any of that, or are you just making up excuses?"

I gasp, "I do *not* make up excuses." I give myself a second to think about it. Okay, so maybe one time. Alright, a few times. "I don't make a habit out of it anyway."

"Yes, you do! You have always come up with reasons not to own up to your actions, and you are always the last to say sorry. You've got to get over that, sweetheart. Admit you made a mistake and get Roban back."

"But is that enough? To say sorry?" I ask. "I really think I messed things up. I'm not sure a simple apology is going to cut it." I can hear my mother talking away from the receiver. It must be Robert. Does he ever leave her alone? "Mom? Are you there?"

My question is received with a crunching crackle as my mother tries to put her phone back to her ear.

"Sorry, honey. It's just Robert," she says. *I knew it.* "If you're unsure, I say do something big. Something he might like."

"Like a painting?" I say.

"Sure, if he likes that sort of thing."

"I think he does," I say, but it sounds more like a question when I say it aloud. "Besides, I don't really have a lot of other skills and I don't have a lot of money."

"I'm sure a painting would be great. Umm... one second," I can hear the muffled sound of voices, one is my mother's whisper and the other is deep but genial. "Okay," she says, "I'll tell her."

I'm impatient with Robert's frequent interruptions. "Mom?"

"Yes, yes, I'm here. So, listen. I've got some big news."

My breathing becomes rapid and my thoughts race. I don't know if I can handle big news. Not from my mom. All I can think is that it's got to be bad. It has to be bad. Her health is probably worse. I'm going to lose my mom. I'm going to lose her...

"Robert and I got engaged," she says frankly.

"What!?" I shriek. "Mom, you can't be serious. You haven't even been dating that long!"

She waits for me to calm down. My head is spinning. I can't believe what I'm hearing.

"Honey, when you get to be my age, you realize that you don't have much time. Life is too short to hesitate. Robert and I love each other, and we want to spend what years we have left together. It's as simple as that. Besides, you insisted that someone be here to take care of me. Why not Robert? Really, if you got to know him, I think you'd really like him."

"But Dad..." I make out, but I can't finish the thought.

"Your dad wouldn't want me to be a martyr forever, Emily. It's been twelve years. We have to move forward with our lives. We can't keep living in the past. He'd want me to be happy. He'd want me to love again. And I am happy. I am in love."

I have to sit with this for a second. I set the phone down

on the kitchen counter and hunch over, trying to catch my breath. My mother is really doing it. She's getting married. Robert is going to be my stepdad. There is nothing I can do to stop it. And maybe that's for the best. She's right, I was insistent that someone be there with her. If Robert really loves her, how can I say no? How could I deny my mother the happiness she deserves?

After I've taken a moment to recover, I put the phone back to my ear.

"Are you sure this is what you want?" I say.

"Yes, honey," she says. "I'm sure. When you're older, maybe you'll understand that we'll all need help someday. It's best to surround yourself with people that love you so that help is there when you need it most. I can't take care of myself anymore. I've had to come to accept that. But Robert loves me anyway. He's happy to help."

"Okay," I say.

"Okay? You mean you're fine with this?"

"Yes," I sigh. For once, I don't feel like fighting. In fact, I find the corner of my lips curled into a small smile. "I'm happy for you. Really."

"Well, this conversation went better than I expected," she laughs. "But listen, I'm late for an appointment. Do something nice for Roban, would you? It's no fun going through life alone."

"I will," I say.

She hangs up.

If my mother of all people can learn to love again, so can I. I just hope it's not too late. I rush to my laptop on the coffee table, open a new tab, and begin searching for the words I can never forget. I already know what I'm going to do.

eighteen

IT TAKES me all morning to prepare, but I am ready to ask for Roban's forgiveness. At least I think I am. I hope my memory doesn't prove faulty, that I can retain the words that I spent hours memorizing.

Something my mother said is paining me, but has given me absolute clarity. It's something both her and Alice have been trying to knock into my head all summer long. But now the summer is over. Today is the autumnal equinox, which I recognize as the time to harvest, to acknowledge growth. It is a rebirth, not just for the earth, but for myself.

God, I have spent so long wallowing in self-pity. I have been selfish and I have been greedy. I thought I was special, like I could do without love, but as my mother has taught me, love is something we can't do without. It makes us better people that strive to be softer, kinder. Roban certainly has made me a better person, sanding the edges of my harsh personality like he was scraping and planing a rough wooden surface. I could be alone. I don't doubt that. But why should I? Aren't I sick of being a victim of my divorce? Wasn't I happier when I was in Roban's company? Yes, yes, all yes.

I grab the painting I made for Roban after our first date. It leans against the tangerine curtains in the dining room, waiting to be displayed if Roban would have it. It's not very big, so I am able to deftly pack it into the back of my car without having to put the seats down. All the while I am mumbling to myself over and over, trying not to forget what needs to be said.

I speed down the road for blocks and blocks, not bothering to slow down for potholes. My alignment will be shot, but this cannot wait any longer. Red and golden leaves bounce off of the hood of the car and slide up the windshield, cast into the sky until they find their final place to settle. Still, I am talking to myself, reciting the same thing until I pull up at the curb to his house with a screeching stop.

I retrieve the painting from the backseat and run to Roban's stoop, ringing the doorbell again and again with the urgency that only I must feel. *What if it's too late?* I shudder at the thought.

The handle of the front door jiggles and it swings wide open. I expect to see Roban, or possibly his housemate Matt, but I am instead surprised by the appearance of a tall, smart-dressed woman with bright red lipstick, a navy blazer, and black suede pumps. Her immaculately curled hair is teased to one side, tumbling down the front of her right shoulder. Put simply, this woman is stunning, and so much more put together than I am in my paint stained yellow paisley dress, and my God, am I wearing flip flops?

"Can Ah help ye?" she says, eyeing me incredulously.

Fuck. She's Scottish, too. She sounds just like Roban does. And then it hits me, this must be Roban's ex-fiance, Sophie.

I think about turning around, running to the car with my painting in hand and driving home to cry into a pillow, but I've come this far. I have to fight for Roban, even if I have to compete with a queenly woman like Sophie.

"Is Roban here? I need to speak with him," I say. "It's urgent."

"One moment," she says, disappearing behind the door and shutting it in my face. Briefly, I think she won't come back, that she won't actually grab Roban. It feels like so long. I shift my weight from one leg to the other, looking around the yard until I hear faint footsteps approaching the door. I brace myself to be met with Sophie once more, but no. The door opens and there is Roban, beautiful as the first day I saw him. He's bundled up in a thick red flannel and his hair is bunched up on the top of his head, with just a few loose hairs framing his face. His beard is longer, thicker somehow, and he looms so much larger than I remember.

"Emily, whit ur ye daein' haur?" he says. I try to ignore Sophie's shadow behind him.

"I—" I stammer, "I wanted to say something to you but I'm not sure how to say it. But I have to try. Please, just listen until I am done." I clear my throat and begin reciting the poem I worked so hard to memorize:

"Oh wert thou in the cauld blast,
On yonder lea, on yonder lea;
My plaidie to the angry airt,
I'd shelter thee, I'd shelter thee:
Or did Misfortune's bitter storms
Around thee blaw, around thee blaw,
Thy bield should be my bosom,
To share it a', to share it a'—"

Roban interrupts me before I can finish the poem, taking the painting from my hands and setting it inside before he clasps my palms in his. Then he smiles and finishes the rest:

"Or were I in the wildest waste,
Sae black and bare, sae black and bare,
The desert were a Paradise,
If thou wert there, if thou wert there.
Or were I monarch o' the globe,
Wi' thee to reign, wi' thee to reign;
The brightest jewel in my crown
Wad be my queen, wad be my queen."

After the last line passes from his lips, he steps toward me and moves his hand to the small of my back. I'm pressed close to his warm, brawny body. I'm afraid to look up, but he tilts my chin up with his other hand until I am gazing up at his familiar glacial blue eyes.

"I've missed ye," he says. "Woods it be alright if Ah kissed ye?"

I nod eagerly as I feel a tear slide down my creased, smiling cheeks. Roban grabs each side of my face and pulls me, slowly, into a deep kiss. His lips are smooth as they graze against mine, his tongue sweet as candy. Our mouths knit and knot together, coaxing, claiming each other as our own. I don't want to let go as he steps back from me, his hands now on my hips.

"Yer Scottish accent is terrible, by th' way," he laughs. "But ye ken hoo much Ah loove Burns."

I laugh, too. I don't even realize that I am still crying, relieved that Roban still wants me like I want him.

"I know I've been awful," I say, "The truth is that I love you. I know I never told you that, and I wish I had much sooner. I pushed you away when I should have been pulling you closer. I blamed you for things I shouldn't have, and for that I am so, so very sorry. I was just scared of falling for someone again, thinking that it would be just like the last time, and I would lose myself in the process. I feared you. I feared that you would try to domesticate me and take my art away from me. But deep down, I knew none of that was true. I guess what I was really afraid of was needing someone else, wanting someone else. I don't need you, Roban, but I want you. I want you around me as much as possible. I'm sorry I was so blind."

Roban's stare is tender. I ask for forgiveness, but he has already given it before he opens his mouth.

"Emily, It's okay. Ah am sorry Ah didne respect yer boondaries. An' Ah am sorry fur th' boys' behaviur. They tauld me whit happened an' Ah was furioos. But ye waur awreddy gone. Ah thooght mebbe Ah shoods chase ye, but 'en Ah thooght mebbe 'at was th' problem. Ah hoped one ay these days ye woods come back sae Ah coods teel ye hoo truly sorry Ah am fur everythin'," he says. "Ah am in loove wi' ye. But ye awreddy knew 'at."

He holds me close, squeezing with his trunk-like arms. I have trouble catching my breath. *He loves me*, I think. But he's right. I think I knew all along.

"Ahem," a woman clears her voice in the doorway. "Roban, who is thes?"

Fuck, I tremble, *I forgot about Sophie*. Suddenly, I am very confused. If Roban loves me, then what is this woman doing in his house? Why would he say all those things, hug and kiss me like he did, in front of her?

"Och, sorry. Ah almost forgot," Roban says. "Ainsley, thes is Emily."

Ainsley? She is the one I saw flash on Roban's phone earlier this summer. This is the woman with whom he is always chatting. I feel a surge of jealousy, a wave of intense emotion: anxiety, anger, confusion. But then I remember that Roban chose me.

Ainsley looks me over, and then her face breaks into a large smile, revealing a crooked front tooth behind her immaculate red lipstick.

"Emily, it's a pleasure tae meit ye. I've heard sae much abit ye," she says, extending her arm toward me.

I shake her hand. Her grip is light and friendly.

"You mean, she's not... Sophie?" I'm very confused.

They both laugh.

"Sophie!? Heavens nae. She's bin gone a lang time. Ah don't expect she'll ever be back," Roban chuckles. It's nice that he can laugh about his broken engagement, but if this isn't Sophie, who the hell is Ainsley? My face is stone.

"Sorry, I still don't understand. Who are you?" I ask sheepishly.

"Apologies. Ah am Roban's sister. Ah am jist haur visitin' fur th' week," says Ainsley.

His sister? I feel so stupid. I'll confess, Roban and I haven't talked much about family this summer. He mentioned his mother's back in Oban and his sister lives in Glasgow, but I never once asked about their names.

"Oh my God," I say, my cheeks flushed. "I thought you might have been..."

"Whit? His girlfriend?" Ainsley giggles.

I nod. My face is hot and I'm sure my pale skin betrays me, because Roban pinches my cheek in jest.

"Yoo've got naethin' tae fear yerself abit frae me, lass. Ye ur th' only one fur me. It's always bin ye."

Roban holds my hand tightly in his.

"Sae yoo're a painter?" Ainsley asks, picking up the painting off of the floor. She observes it for a long time, longer than most people. Normally, people just glance at my work, but I'm afraid they never really see me. I feel self-conscious the longer she stares, but finally she looks at me and says, "Thes is excellent wark, Emily. Rilly excellent. Ah loove whit yoo've dain wi' th' colors haur, th' contrest atween th' soft pinks an' purples an' th' brash red. There's a lot ay emotion haur. Ye shoods be very prood ay yer wark."

"Thank you," I say, and I mean it. She seems to really *get it*. She understands the painting, even if she wasn't there that night at the aviary. "Are you a big art fan then?"

Roban and Ainsley both break into hysterical laughter, but I'm afraid the joke is lost on me.

"Sorry, did I miss something?" I ask.

Ainsley composes herself while Roban still stifles his laughter behind a clenched fist.

"Ye coods indeed say Ah am an art fan," she says.

Roban punches her arm.

"She's bein' modest. Ainsley is an art dealer," says Roban. I audibly gasp. Not just in my head, but embarrassingly and loudly gasp. "Ah meant tae teel ye eventually. Ah jist wanted tae make sure ye liked me fur me an' nae mah sister. That's aw."

"Do you really think I would do such a thing?" I say. I am frozen, still recovering from the shock of this news.

"Nae noo, but when we first met an' Ah foond out ye waur a painter, Ah thooght it best remain a secrit until th' reit time," he says. "Ah hope ye can forgife me."

I look up at his loving, scruffy face. "Of course I forgive you, Roban. I understand."

"Ah am a wee upsit it's taken thes lang tae meit ye, Emily. Roban has bin textin' me photos ay yer wark. Yoo're rilly talented," Ainsley chimes in. "It rilly is an honur."

I blush. I've never really been praised for my work like this, not by someone like Ainsley. I knew I wanted her to like me the moment she answered the door, but now that Roban's secret is out, my knees are weak and I feel like I might faint. An art dealer really likes my work! I take deep breaths and try to calm myself down. I want to play it cool but I am just so damn excited.

"You're too kind," I say, turning away so that my hair can mask my flushing face.

Ainsley sucks in her breath, turning to exit. "I'll leave ye two lovebirds be. But Emily, don't be a stranger." She casts me a wink and disappears into the house.

"Your sister seems nice," I say. I give Roban's hand a squeeze.

Roban twirls me toward him and holds me close, staring straight into my eyes. I want to look away, feeling a bit embarrassed, but I am so enchanted by him that I couldn't avert my gaze if I tried.

"Ah am glad ye loch 'er. Ah might nae git tae see them 'at often, but mah family is very important tae me," he says. "But Christ, Ah am glad she is gone. Ah jist want tae be aloyn wi' ye. I've missed ye."

"I've missed you, too," I say.

"Noo, listen. Ah ken ye waur apprehensife tae be wi' me. Ah ken hoo hard it's bin fur ye, given everythin' yoo've bin through. But Ah hae tae know... ur ye rilly done wi' David?"

His face is pained, the corners of his eyes creased, his mouth downcast. I can feel his heartbeat on my chest.

"Yes," I say. "I am done with David. Forever."

"Ur ye sure? Ah ken he offered tae help ye wi' yer maw an'—"

"I'm sure," I say, "My mom and I will be fine without him."

Roban presses his lips to mine. "Ah am sae glad tae hear ye say 'at."

I stuff my hands in his back pockets as we rock side to side. The autumn sun is shining above us, dappled light glistening through the trees. I want to stay in this moment forever, just Roban and I holding each other close. All of the tension between us cleared, all of my apprehensions gone. For once, I think things will be better. I've never fallen this hard—not over anyone, even David, because this is pure love. There are no expectations. No conditions. Just him and me, held helplessly in one another's fierce adoration.

"Teel me ye loove me again," he says.

"I love you, Roban Campbell," I smile.

Roban raises his hand to my face slowly, gently caressing the fuzz on my cheeks. It takes all of my willpower not to kiss him, to stay in this moment for as long as I can. He smooths my hair behind my ears and plants a delicate kiss right on my forehead.

"An' Ah loove ye, Emily Williams."

"What did I ever do to deserve you?" I whisper. I can feel a lump in my throat.

"Naethin'. Ye didne hae tae," he says in a low voice. "Noo let's go inside an' hae a drink. Ah want Ainsley tae hear aw abit yer art."

nineteen

I SMOOTH my favorite black sweater dress over the length of my body and turn to Roban.

"Does this look alright?" I say. There are knots in my stomach and I can feel my pulse in my skull. I'll admit, I'm feeling quite nervous.

"Ye look very bonnie, lass," he says, kissing me lightly on the cheek.

"You don't think I went too over the top with drinks and hors d'oeuvres, do you?"

My friends and family should arrive any minute now to celebrate the updated house. Nothing like the last second to be asking these kinds of questions.

"Ah think it will be a very classy hoosewarmin' party," he says. "That's whit ye wanted, isnae it?"

"Yes, but I'm truly afraid that I've lost my mind this time," I laugh.

"It will be braw. Deep breaths," Roban says. He inhales deeply, urging me to breathe with him. I take in a mouthful of air, but before I get the chance to exhale, the doorbell rings. The first guests appear to have arrived.

In a hurry, I slip on some heeled booties and dash to the door, letting the guests inside and inviting them to help themselves to food and drink.

Although I am frenzied, Alice taps me on the shoulder. "Emily, I hardly recognized you. You don't get dolled up often, but when you do... Serious knockout!" she cheers.

"Well, I thought I ought to look a little more put together if I'm going to celebrate finishing up the house," I say, nudging her with my elbow. "Thank you for helping by the way. The house looks marvelous."

And it really does. If people think I am unrecognizable in a black party dress, then they will be even more astonished by the new decor for the house. All of David's modern furniture is gone, down to the very last barstool. Over the last few weeks, Alice and Roban helped me pack everything up and sell it to a second-hand marketplace. Though I detest David's style, I'm glad it was trendy enough to fetch me a pretty dollar. The store bought all of it, and with the money they gave me, I was able to refurnish the entire home: vintage wooden side tables; kitchen cupboards that Alice and I upscaled with a fresh layer of vibrant paint and new hardware; feminine rugs and runners throughout the house to protect the refinished hardwood floors; and so much more. I couldn't have done all of this without Alice and Roban. For once, I walk in my house without feeling the spirit of my dead marriage. Instead, there is light, love, and a playfulness that I had been missing for the last decade.

Perhaps a wiser person would have told me to just sell the house, but I love my neighborhood. I like being able to walk to the bar and the coffee shop, the restaurants on the corner, the kitschy storefronts down the boulevard. I like my tree-lined streets and the cute exteriors of the homes next door. I firmly believe that when something is broken, it can be fixed (not my marriage, but that is beside the point). Rather than packing up and moving, I started my new life with just a few brush strokes.

"It was my pleasure to help," Alice says. "After all, I live here, too."

I laugh as I let in more guests, leading them to the kitchen so they can grab some nourishment.

"I guess you could also thank me for hooking you up with Roban," she winks.

"You did *not* hook me up with Roban, Alice."

"Hey, I pushed you every step of the way. You kicked and screamed the whole time, but look at you now!" she says. Alice looks at me with warmth as Roban approaches with two drinks in his hands: one for him, one for me. "I'm just glad to see you so happy."

"Well, thank you, Alice, for the push," I giggle. "It was worth it."

Roban's cheeks flush. I can see it even with his dark beard. As Alice nods and leaves to help entertain the guests, I turn to Roban and grab him by the sides of his belt, swaying to the music playing, even though it's hard to hear over the boisterous conversations in the next room.

"Seems loch people loch whit yoo've dain wi' th' hoose," he says.

"The house is so far from my mind right now." And it's true. Even though we are surrounded by friends, all I can think about is how happy I am that Roban is here with me.

"Then whit is oan yer min'" he asks, nuzzling close, swaying with me back and forth.

I kiss him gently on the lips.

"I am just so lucky that you gave me another chance."

His lips glide over mine, enticing me forward with his

steady hands on my hips. I try to ignore the presence of our guests, but I can feel their occasional stares.

"Easy, tiger," I say. "We have a party to go to."

"Och aye, but Ah cannae help 'at Ah want ye reit noo," he whispers. His hand drifts from my hips to my buttocks just as there comes a loud knock on the door.

"Later," I say, wriggling out of his hands. "I promise."

When I open the door, I am surprised to see that my mother and Robert have made it to the party. During one of our weekly phone calls, I mentioned that I was having a gathering to celebrate the new space. She sounded interested, so I invited her, but I seriously didn't think she would drive all the way from Moab to attend.

"Mom! Robert. You came!" I exclaim. I give my mother a big hug and stand aside so she can come in.

"Anything to get me out of the house," she says.

Robert outstretches his hand to shake mine. I acquiesce. His gray hair is combed back and he's wearing a button-up shirt, a playful tie, and slacks. It's not that fancy of a party, but I appreciate that he made the effort.

"It's nice to see you," Robert says. "Linda talks about you all of the time. You have a beautiful home."

"Thanks," I say. "Please, come on in. There are drinks and hors d'oeuvres in the kitchen."

Robert helps my mother inside and lets her go off into the party. To my surprise, he stops to chat with me.

"Emily, do you have a minute?" he asks politely.

"Sure," I say apprehensively.

"Linda told me she told you about the engagement," he says.

"Oh."

"Look, I think we started on the wrong foot. I just want to say, I know it must be difficult accepting me into your life since your father passed, but I really hope you will take the time to get to know me. You don't have to call me Dad, you're in your thirties for Christ's sake. I just really love your mom and I want you to know that I will take great care of her, no matter what." His face is stern but gentle. He is kind of handsome for his age. I can see why my mother likes him.

"I appreciate that, Robert," I say. My tone is genuine—a far cry from when I met him at the beginning of summer. "I never got to apologize for how I acted all those months ago. I'm really sorry. I'm just protective of my mom and I don't want her to get hurt."

"I completely understand," he says. "My mother remarried when I was just ten years old. I hated my step dad. I didn't like anyone new coming into the picture. I think as children, even adult children, we're easily disrupted when something or someone interrupts life as usual. I know I may have caused some disruption between you and Linda, but I hope you'll see how happy we are together. Maybe that will change your mind?"

"You may have been a point of contention, but believe me when I say there is nothing that I treasure more than my mom's happiness. If you make her happy, I'm happy. You know?" I blink at him. He's right, he'll never take the place of my dad. But I really do want my mom to be happy, and if that means taking another shot at love, there is likely no better man for her than Robert.

"Thank you," Robert says. He dabs the corner of his glossy eye with his tie. "That means a lot to me. Now," he clears his throat, gathering his composure, "You better go find Linda. I'm sure you have a lot to talk about."

He smiles at me. I smile back and turn toward the kitchen, ambling toward the din in the other room.

As I enter the kitchen, Roban and Alice raise their glasses, prompting all of my other friends and family to do the same.

"Tae Emily an' Alice's bonnie new home," Roban toasts.

Everyone cheers.

I fuss with my dress and look down at my booties. "Thank you all so much for being here," I say. "I really feel like you are all welcome here for once, like this is *my* home. And I couldn't have done it without Alice and Roban, so," I lift my glass to them.

The guests follow suit and clink each other's glasses as I pull my mother aside.

"Mom, you really didn't have to come all this way for a silly housewarming party."

She scoffs. "Oh, please. I haven't been back in Salt Lake City in a long time, but you know I'd like to see you more often. It's time to put the past behind us," she smiles. "Besides, I can't expect you to visit me every time, can I?"

"Only if Robert is willing to drive," I say sternly. "Congratulations on the engagement, by the way. Sorry I didn't react better when you told me. It's fabulous news."

"I know you'd prefer that I just take care of myself forever, but you know that's not an option anymore," she says. "It will be good, having Robert around. And I know you'll be around, too. I'm not upset about the diagnosis. In the end, I'm sure I'll be fine."

I admire her optimism. It makes me feel like maybe my mother being diagnosed with Parkinson's isn't the end of the world. But I know we have mountains to climb, but I'll be there for her, whatever she needs. Robert will, too.

"I apologized to Robert," I confess. "I understand why you like him. He's very nice."

"He is. I love him, Emily. I know it seems like our

engagement was fast, but we're getting older and we don't have the time nor the patience to play games. When you love someone, you just sort of... go for it," she says. "Never be afraid to take a chance on love. Even when it hurts, it's worth it." She nods toward Roban. "You never told me this guy you were seeing was so handsome. And I love his accent! Where's he from? Ireland?"

"Scotland, Mom."

"Alright, Scotland. But you ought to hang onto him. He's one of the good ones. I can tell." She pinches my cheek.

I gently remove her hand from my face. "That's what people keep telling me."

"I'm glad you changed your mind," she says.

"About what?"

"About Robert. And Roban. About everything. You've changed since your divorce." She eyes me up and down. "For the better, I promise. I didn't hate David, it's just that you never seemed happy with him, even in the beginning. But looking at you now, gosh! It makes me so proud of the woman you've become."

"Mom, stop," I say, blushing. I kind of want to cry. It's been a long time since I've heard praise from my mother. Perhaps I have David to blame for that. Or maybe myself. "I do *feel* different. I don't know. My art is going really well, I am absolutely ga-ga over Roban, and I live with my best friend in a beautiful house. I am very lucky."

"Well, thank God for Alice. She's been a godsend all these years. You need someone other than me to knock some sense into you." She knocks lightly on the side of my head, cackling all the while.

"If she tells you she set me up with Roban, it isn't true," I say, sure that Alice is telling the entire party lies about her role in my flourishing relationship. "I nabbed him all by myself. I may have needed a little encouragement, but that is beside the point."

"I'm glad either way," my mom says. "Now, I'll let you get back to your party. Robert and I will mingle and I'll help myself to some bruschetta. Love the house, by the way. It's very... *you.*"

I kiss my mom on the cheek and return to entertaining my guests. The evening is lovely, and I am ecstatic that Roban got the opportunity to meet my mom. She's a wonderful woman. My heroine, through and through. Without her, there would be no art, no house, no love. I am indebted to her for so many reasons, but mostly I am glad that she demonstrated that it's possible to find love after loss. I wasn't so sure about that myself. In fact, it was my primary struggle during years of therapy. But now that I've escaped my loveless marriage and I adore someone who adores me for who I really am and who I could be (not just who they want me to be), I feel free.

Independence, I've learned, is not lost when you fall for someone. Love does not require that you give up your goals and aspirations. Love should inspire you to be better, and I feel like I am better now: less selfish, more attuned to other people's needs. Roban has made the bitterness I carried with me for so many years disappear. For once, I feel like anything is possible and I'm not afraid to ask for help.

Without the help of my boyfriend, my friend, and my mother, I would still be trapped in this dark abyss. Humans need connection. I need connection. Now, with the freedom to surround myself with people I actually love, I am truly happy.

The guests linger, talking, pouring endless glasses of wine, and dancing to the latest hits on the stereo. Alice does a great job of noticing when I am overwhelmed and steps in to help. Roban takes my hand and dances with me in the corner of the kitchen, stepping on my toes here and there, but I don't mind. To be close to him is enough.

"Thank you," I whisper, "For everything."

"It's nae problem, lass. Ah dornt feel loch Ah did anythin' at aw," he says, twirling me in a circle. "Come. Ah want tae shaw ye somethin'."

Roban leads me to the living room and opens up the curtains. The sun is setting, casting a pink and purple sunset not unlike the one we saw at the aviary all those months ago. But in the dusk light, Roban points to the chokecherry sapling in the front yard.

"Thaur, th' tree," he says. "It's growin' wee flowers. Dae ye see them?"

"I do. They're beautiful."

I squeeze Roban's hand tightly, leading him to the front porch. Together, side by side, we sit on the porch swing, watching the last of the light sink below the horizon.

epilogue

ROBAN RUBS my back as we wait at baggage claim. It took more than ten hours to fly to Glasgow International Airport, but we are both so happy to finally be here.

"Ah ne'er thooght Ah woods be back in Scootlund," Roban says.

"It'll be fine," I say. "We aren't even in Oban. We're both strangers here."

We grab our bags off of the carousel, waiting patiently until they round the turn closest to us. I'm walking so fast that I practically leave Roban behind in the airport, but once he notices my pace he jumps in step with me, which isn't hard for him considering his long legs.

"Slaw doon, speed racer. We'll gie tae th' gallery soon enough," he says. But I can't seem to slow my steps. I am darting out the doors and into the pickup lane to wait for a black taxi to take us to our hotel. Once the doors close behind me, I am greeted with the sweet, icy air of early Spring. I hail down a cab quickly. I am eager to wash the sweat from the sweltering flight off of my body, change into something nice, and go straight to the gallery. Ainsley will be expecting us.

"EMILY! Roban! Ah am sae glad ye made it in one piece," Ainsley coos as we approach the glass double doors of her gallery. She is standing in front of them, preventing us from entering too hastily. I want to push her aside and see what she's done, but I remind myself to keep my cool. This is months in the making. Having constant contact with Ainsley as I shipped my paintings overseas and planning opening night at the gallery has been a lot of work, mostly on her part. I am appreciative of what she has done for me, so I muster a little bit of patience for these last few moments before I see the gallery in person.

"Emily haur was sae excited she didne sleep a wink oan th' plane. In fact, ance we freshened up at th' hotel, she insisted we come straight haur," Roban says. Ainsley kisses us both on the cheek.

I punch his arm in jest. "So, I'm a little excited for my first gallery opening. Give me a break." I can feel myself grinning ear to ear. It's painful, but not forced. I am truly, genuinely ecstatic that it's finally happening. I am standing on the streets of downtown Glasgow before my own art gallery. It's taken years to get to this point in my career. It's all I ever wanted.

"Ur ye ready tae see it?" Ainsley asks. She does a little dance to entice me, as if I need to be enticed.

"Yes! Yes! Stop teasing me, Ainsley, and open the door!" I groan.

Roban rubs my back gently and nudges me forward as Ainsley unlocks the door. I take a deep breath. This is it.

Ainsley holds the door open as Roban and I enter the gallery. It's dark, but I can still see the paintings closest to the window. My paintings.

She flicks on the light and suddenly I am overwhelmed by walls upon walls of my work, hanging for the delight of anyone who might view it. Seriously. I am stunned. I have no words.

"Dae ye loch it?" Ainsley asks. Her voice wobbles a bit, as if she is just as anxious about this whole thing as I am.

I bite my tongue. There are so many things I want to say as I walk along the walls and see my artwork displayed somewhere other than my home or a vendor booth at an arts festival. This gallery is so... posh. The floors are stained a deep, dark shade of brown—almost black—and there are beautiful plants in gorgeous vases all over the room: monsteras, fiddle-leaf figs, and peace lilies, all reaching their leaves toward the crystal chandelier dangling in the middle of the ceiling. On the back wall, front and center, is my painting that I made for Roban. It's the only piece that is not for sale: it's simply here for viewing purposes. I trace my hand along the edge of the canvas.

"Emily?" Roban asks, an edge of concern in his tone. "Ur ye alright?"

I can feel a tear trickle down my cheek and into the corner of my mouth.

"I—I love it," I say. I rush to Ainsley, who is still standing tentatively by the door, and swing my arms around her neck, pulling her into a tight hug. "Thank you."

"Och, honey. Dornt thenk me. It's ye Ah shoods be thankin'," she laughs.

"It looks better than I ever dreamed it would," I confess. I have been dreaming of this moment nearly all of my life. Regardless of how many times I've tried to replay this moment in my head, it never came out clear. My imagination was blurry, probably because part of me had resigned to accept that this would never happen for me. But here it is, all around me, years of work that I couldn't ever sell.

"Jist wait. Tomorrow night will be fantastic. Th' guests will aw be eager tae meit ye," Roban says. Ainsley nods in agreement. "Yoo've dain it, Emily. We're haur. Yoo've dain it."

I wrap my arm around Roban's waist and we take it in for a moment longer.

He's right. I've done it. I've really done it.

THE END

acknowledgments

For those who have read my first book, this story might be shockingly different. That's because I wanted to tell a more vulnerable, personal story about love and independence, exploring how the two are not mutually exclusive.

This book consumed me for many months, during which time I was broke and unemployed. However, my wonderful husband supported me, allowing me to concentrate on writing this story. I hope someday I can return the favor and give him the time and space he needs to pursue his passion, but for now, we are both working stiffs.

As always, I must thank my best friend, Amanda, for holding my hand through this journey: not just the one I took writing this book, but my entire journey since our last year of college. The last decade has been a rollercoaster, and I appreciate her being there for me as I tried to find my place in this world. Even now, I don't know what I am doing or where I belong, but her friendship makes it easier. She reads my work even if no one else ever does. A huge thank you goes out to her for keeping me dedicated to my art.

This was a difficult story to tell and I hope I did it justice. I hope it touches anyone who has had to start over after a failed relationship, who has taken on the role of caretaker, who has chosen the daring path of the artist. I know it's not easy.

about the author

Sara Wetmore is an award-winning author based in Salt Lake City, Utah. She studied creative writing at Lindenwood University, where she earned her MFA. Her work has appeared in The Write Launch, Shadowed Hourglass, Adelaide magazine, and others. When she's not writing, you can catch her reading a book, traveling the world with her husband, or playing with her two cats.

facebook.com/sarawetmorewriting
twitter.com/writing_sara
instagram.com/writingsara
goodreads.com/sarawetmore

CPSIA information can be obtained
at www.ICGtesting.com
Printed in the USA
LVHW100021160222
711212LV00013B/574

9 781737 642923